Love and Loss

Trinity Ambrose

I dedicate this book to my unwavering family who constantly encourage me to keep trying and my kids who add magic and wonder to my every day life.

Chapter One
THE BEGINNING

FRESH honeysuckle perfumed the late spring air as the family's blue station wagon roared down the dark highway towards home. The Kelleys, a young couple and their three-year old daughter, were heading home after a long night of visiting with friends. Old rock and roll favorites from the Eagles genre played lightly in the background as the parents talked quietly to avoid waking the sleeping child, weary from the drive. Everyone was eager to get home. Sleepiness crept over the occupants of the car as they continued down the highway. There really wasn't much to look out at to keep them occupied, just pavement and mountains. This part of the Parkway was more scenic; peaceful.

Flecks of gray and black scattered across the sky as the stars mingled with the clouds, like movie stars mingling with visitors at a luxurious party. The road was cold and black, stretching out in front of them like an endless sea with only their headlights to guide the way. When they first spotted the semi, they were relieved; relieved to see that there was still light in the darkness regardless of its shape and sudden speed. Joe was the first to notice that the semi didn't seem to be handling very well.

Frank Holtz, the driver of the 18-wheeler, was just coming home from a drop in Tennessee. Now all he had to do was haul his trailer and another home to Cynthiana. The last few miles had seemed like a dream to him. He kept rubbing his hazel eyes, trying to fight the drowsiness. Frank too had thought the idea of sleep was comforting, images of his soft bed and cool sheets plagued his mind. He rolled down the window to fight the relaxing warmth, and allowed the cold air to tussle his dark chestnut hair, streaked with gray; his shaggy beard tickled with the breeze.

'So warm,' he thought, regretting the whiskey he had partaken in back at the truck stop. '*It will warm you up and make you feel better,*' a little voice inside him had said. He knew how it would affect him but he just wanted to make the voice shut up. Frank flashed to a vision of his drunken father staggering around the house after a long night's binge.

"A man should never drink that much on an empty stomach…" Famous last words said by a drunk before being violently ill in front of the boy. He wished he had heeded that advice. The yellow lines on the asphalt floated and swirled like a ribbon in the wind. Frank was trying desperately to chase the ribbon like a cat in a cartoon chasing a string until he reaches his comical doom. That made him smile in spite of himself, but that smile faded as he looked out the open window. The trees that were flying past the truck were making him nauseous. Oh, why had he drunk? He just had one, right? Maybe two? His head was fuzzy and he couldn't remember. Panic set in as his vision became blurry, and he pulled the steering wheel hard to the right hoping to get off the road. The rig swerved out of his control as if pulled from him. What the hell! His arms pin-wheeled, weaving back and forth as he tried to gain command back over the rig. It felt like he was fighting some strange force that had a hold of his trailer and was shaking it like a child with a toy.

"Why is this happening?" he asked aloud, voice shaking. All he heard in return was a deep crazed laugh that echoed off the walls of his skull. The familiar sound made him flash back to a few weeks ago as memories of a dark hotel in another state that smelled faintly of sweat and blood emerged. He could see the blood that covered his hands as he had run out the door. So deep...cut so deep. He had sprinted headlong into the pouring rain, trying to out run that crazed voice.

Beams of light shown through the darkness, bringing him back to the present. He fought against the dark laugh, now taking control of his body. His foot, acting on its own free will, pressed down on the accelerator, bringing the rig barreling ever faster down the road towards the blue station wagon. Fear rose in him causing him to break out in beads of sweat. '*It's happening again!*' he thought. He questioned if this vehicle was even real out here in the middle of nowhere. Had he completely lost it? His body and mind were not his own so not too hard to believe that he would imagine another car out in the dark just so he didn't have to feel so alone.

His first impression of the Kelley's wagon was the fact that it was so small and seemed to be coming upon him too fast. The next few minutes were fuzzy and unreal, almost as if they happened to someone else. Joe Kelley knew they were in for some trouble. Fear clawed at him, thinking of what would happen if they didn't get out of the way of the hurling mass of steel. He was frazzled, trying to think of what to do, as he tried slowing down to look for a spot to pull off. But he realized there was nowhere to go. On either side of the road, there was a 15-foot drop from pavement to earth and no guardrails to help them on this particular part of the Cumberland Parkway. Joe looked at his beautiful wife and before they could buckle-up for the impact, the semi clipped the front driver's side and put them in a spin.

As the car spun fast and out of control, Mrs. Sunny Kelley's slight form was flung from the window. Later, the coroner wouldn't be able to determine whether the collision of her head with the glass or the blunt trauma of being thrown 100 yards from the wreck site had killed her. Joe's body had remained in the car, his neck snapped by the airbag when he turned his head to look back at the baby. There was no one left capable of controlling the car as it spun freely till it stopped. In his truck, Frank awoke not knowing how he had come to a halt but lifting his head from the wheel, he took a look. The cargo trailer was still attached. Good sign. He didn't seem to be hurt besides a small trickle of blood running down his face. As he reached for the door handle, he heard the first signs of life...a baby crying. His heart skipped a beat. What happened? Had he blacked out? He remembered the beams of light and losing control then blank. Looking at his side mirror, he could barely make out the form of a woman's still body; tattered and broken. Not more blood, not again, he begged. This was only a movie. It had to be, he told himself. Steven Spielberg will jump out of the bushes and say cut any minute. Had to be, surely? He could just make out the taillights of a vehicle through the dust and smoke dangling off the side of the road. Had he hit someone? The woman's chest was moving right? He must not be able to see it. He could visualize the woman alive gasping for air, saying he did nothing wrong, all is fine.

He hadn't done anything, he wasn't the one in control! Who kept making him do these things? Frank smacked his head several times hoping to reveal answers that way. He opened the driver's side door, preparing himself for what he might find. He could see better now through the fog; the car was a station wagon and it was teetering back and forth on the edge of the highway making a horrible metal grinding noise. Any minute now, the car and its contents would spill to the rocks. There was a silhouette of a body hunched over in the front seat, surely they were still breathing? Conflicted, Frank thought of what he should do. All this blood on his hands! His chest seized as his breath came in sharp inhales. Maybe this isn't a movie? He scrambled back into the cab, threw the rig into drive, and booked it down the road in pure terror and disbelief. Nothing but dust and the sound of crying remained in the semi's wake.

In the back seat of the car, still buckled in, Josephine Kelley didn't understand why no one was comforting her. Crying and scared, the gentle rocking of the car started to sooth her unhappiness. She looked up and saw Mommy and Daddy beaming in at her from outside the car. Both were surrounded by a soft glow. Mommy had a tear in her eye and dad seemed to be having difficulty holding his head up to look down at his little one. Her cries turned to giggles as her parent's spirits lifted the car and straightened it on the road. They lowered it slowly to the ground and it barely thumped. She reached her little hand out to her Mommy who waved to her one last time as Dad put a comforting arm around her smiling at his child; their reason to stay behind. Looking at her parents for the last time unbeknown to her, Josephine was happy.

It's funny how a newspaper article can take such a tragic event, something that rips families and lives apart and condense it down to facts and figures.

Tragic Accident Claims Two, Infant Only Survivor

The first witness on the scene claims to have only seen the family's blue station wagon on the side of the road when he happened upon the accident. The vehicle lights were left on but the driver's side had been badly beaten. The witness claims if not for the lights he would have missed it in the dark. After investigating the car, one Larry Flinch noticed a small baby clapping its hands, still buckled in the back seat. The father's body, draped down towards the child in one last attempt to comfort her; the mother laid lifeless yards away.

After the tragedy was reported, we contacted Mr. Flinch and asked him what his recollection of the accident was. "Well, of course I called the police right away but being by myself, I didn't know what to do with the toddler. After seeing she was unharmed, I stood right outside her window until help arrived. I was scared to move her after what she must have been through. She didn't seem scared at all considering; such a brave kid." Indeed, this sole survivor was found to be unscathed and was immediately taken away by Social Services where they will see if there is a next of kin.

The parents, later said to be Mr. Joe and Sunny Kelley, have no family in the area that they have found as of yet but the police are still looking into the matter. If you have any information about this accident or relatives to the Kelley family, please contact the Cumberland Co. police department. No one has come forth in what is now being called a "hit and run" but police have evidence that they wish not to discuss at this time. This reporter was truly heart broken by the sight of the wreckage out on HWY 5 but out of this great loss there is still a life that was spared and it makes you feel that God must really have a plan for this sole survivor.

Chapter Two
NEW BEGINNING

"JO, were you listening to me?"

I snapped my head back to face her. "Sorry Sarah, I must have dozed off there. What were you saying?" I shook my head. Quit daydreaming, I told myself.

"I was talking about the beach. You do remember what a beach is, don't you Josephine?" She looked at me questioningly, hands resting on her hips. I just nodded my head, knowing that her using my "real" name meant that she was on a rant that shouldn't be disturbed. Her blue eyes were bunched up in a disgruntled look. Sarah always got that look about her when she's concerned, but then again Sarah always worried; mostly about me. I wouldn't say she worries completely over nothing. It's hard when your best friend tells you she can see ghosts. Sometimes I think I freak her out with talk about death and the beyond. You know all that science fiction crap you see on TV? Except I see it, like in *real* life. It's everywhere. Momma D, our foster mother, always had the same questioning expression whenever I tried to talk to her about "things", but my thoughts were disturbed as Sarah continued. "Okay, we have decided to go to the beach in Mississippi, and then leave for Mardi Gras before booking it back home to prepare for our return to school, right?" She was counting each point off on her hand and she still had fingers to spare, so I waited patiently for her to continue. After a long awkward silence, I figured she wanted a response.

"You worry too much, it'll be fine!" I threw my hands up and started towards the kitchen to get another bottle of water. There was no point in trying to calm her, years of growing up and living together had taught me that much. Besides, leaving her in charge of the itinerary left me free to goof off till my exams tomorrow. Shimmering rays of light poured in through the patio doors, broken by the swaying trees outside. They danced across the floor like little pixies fluttering amongst flowers. It had turned out to be a beautiful morning for March despite the threats of snow we had earlier in the month. You could really tell spring was in the air. Sarah went on about Spring Break while I continued to the fridge. I walked past the little window over the sink. The kitchen was much sunnier than the living room so conversation or lack thereof, was a little more bearable. I just loved the little flower box we had put on the windowsill. It really made the apartment feel homey. It hadn't been much to look at when we moved in together to attend Brown University.

Sarah broke into my thoughts again. "Besides, I'm not worried, just cautious. I don't want to drive all the way down there and then remember, I left my credit card or something here. I want to be prepared! You know me."

"Yeah, I know." I hid my eye roll as I reached down into the fridge to retrieve my bottle. Since we had been thrown together at the age of nine, I had known she was always going to be the "organized" one. Even when we shared a room in grade school, you could tell the line down the middle of the room. That's probably why she went into accounting. I, on the other hand, like excitement and adventure. I could never sit down and plan what I'm going to do in the next 10 years. Since attending Brown, I have changed majors twice. That went over real well with my Advisor. She's probably a sour puss to everybody.

I looked across the breakfast nook for another distraction and found the pictures hanging on the wall of our high school graduation. Sarah went on about the agenda for our trip but Damien's smile gleamed from the collage of photos, beckoning me. The picture had been taken on our fourth official date at the Big Hill Park. I thought about the proposal after that night. We were by the swings having a romantic dinner on a quilt. The sun had just started to set in the distance and I had managed the whole meal without getting food on me. A small miracle to say in the least. He had gotten down on one knee and told me that he couldn't think of anyone else that he wanted to spend his life with. A life filled with drama what with the dead following me around, I reminded him. Of course we hadn't been together all that time without sharing our deepest, darkest secrets; mine being of course my 'affliction' as I liked to call it. He resisted at first, thinking I was just trying to get a reaction out of him or something. Maybe he thought I was attention seeking or just on my period; who knows but the truth came pretty swift afterwards.

Fortunately for me, not so much for Damien, his pervert female neighbor had passed recently and was totally stalking him. I had caught her a few times out of the corner of my eye at school, darting out of the boys' gym locker rooms, looking hot and bothered as a ghost can be. Usually, I would find her fanning herself with this huge mischief grin by the bleachers and she would just put her finger up to her lips like she was shushing me and disappear. So creepy. It's moments like those that I'm glad I can't hear the ghosts. Lord only knows how scarred for life I would be by now! I describe this 'hungry' apparition to him in great detail and he stopped in his tracks. Instead of continuing to mock me, he turned with a serious look on his face; completely silent. At the time I didn't know she was *his* neighbor, I just thought she gave him more attention than the rest because, in my opinion, he was the hottest guy in school. Still didn't give her any right to walk behind him like she was trying to squeeze his butt in between classes but what ya going to do? She was dead, let her have her freak flag. I spared him that last part out of pity since I had just dropped a bombshell that 'I see dead people' and I didn't think his now fragile mind could take much more. I watched as the color returned to his face and he reached for the nearest chair close to him. I comforted him the only way I knew how, by sitting in silence, avoiding any direct eye contact.

He did come around not long after that, having had time to process (I was totally waiting by the phone freaking out for days). Young people with their internet and stuff; probably wasn't even the weirdest thing he saw that week. His acceptance of me made us inseparable. A girl would have to be crazy to run from a boy like that! Or the boy would have to be crazy not to run from me? Well, either way, it worked out and we were best friends for a little over two years before we decided to take it up a notch.

I was longing for the smell of his after-shave. I really did need this vacation! Damien and I could talk about our future over gorgeous sands and clear waters. I'm sure Sarah will be too busy entertaining Damien's brother Steve, to care about what we'd be doing. It seemed the two were getting pretty serious about one another. Steve was more of the macho type than the sensitive type like Damien. Their personalities may have been different but they both had similar physics; burley men with dark blue eyes that twinkled whenever they were excited. So cute! Damien's dark hair hung loosely past his ears and Steve's sandy blonde hair was cut military short and neat (I'd often made fun of him for it). They both had lovely tans that would stay all year even though they never went to the beach. Just lucky I guess. Thinking of Damien again only made me smile as I looked to Sarah, (still going on about something), pretending to be interested. I took a long drink of my water, like I was deeply contemplating what ever thought she was having, and made a trail around her to the sink to finish up the morning dishes.

She finally stopped her rambling and threw her arms in the air in desperation as she turned on her heel and stormed off to her room; probably to make her final preparations. I chuckled to myself as my mind wandered off again. I was gazing into space, having another pleasant thought, when suddenly a flash blinded me and I dropped the plate in the sink with a loud clank. A man's pale face with scars across, all draped in black, emerged in front of me like in many of my dreams. This can't be right. I'm not dreaming now. I occasionally remembered my dreams, especially the recurring nightmares with him playing the star role. Who was he? How was he coming to me while I was awake? I could feel the fear ravage my body as I shook. Does he have something to do with my curse? If so, then why do I feel so threatened by him? His mouth moved and a chill went down my spine like someone had raked their hand down it. All he was doing was smiling at me, a row of crooked teeth showing, faded and discolored. I closed my eyes tight and tried to push the man from my mind with thoughts of Damien (anything positive and not dark and lurking in front of me should work). I looked from side to side through half squinted eyes. No sign of the man anywhere. That memory alone was still so fresh in my mind that once I opened my eyes, the figure was gone, and all that remained was the smell of honeysuckle. How odd? I had overcome the nightmare once more.

"And stay down," I said aloud and chuckled to myself. I shouldn't be so arrogant. It worked this time and I didn't have a clue what to do if things got worse. How was it that my nightmare was able to manifest itself? For the last two months, his face had haunted me. God knows I can't tell anyone about it. They already think I'm crazy enough! Could this be a new curse I've developed? Maybe a vision of someone I've yet to meet? That would be new. When I was little, it was a rabid dog that kept attacking me in my dreams. The dog had burnt amber eyes and the blackest coat I had ever seen. Sometimes he would cry out to me in a man's voice. Luckily, I haven't met it yet.

At one time in my life, I had no happy memories to fight the bad man away. I thought I would just give up and let the fear take over me, but there always seemed to be a little voice inside my head urging me on, in spite of my misery. Strangely enough, the voice seemed familiar and it too left behind the scent of honeysuckle. '*Better think of something else before he comes back,*' I told myself. Happy thoughts. I thought about Peter Pan and the stories Mamma D always read to 'her children' at night. I closed my eyes and remembered the feel of the colorful rug that we would sit on, with a fire crackling in the distance like a crazed animal trying to escape its fiery cage. Children would be scattered about the room, all leaning forward, lingering on each word that dropped from her mouth. 'Happily ever after' seemed to be the ending to all of the stories regardless of what the book said. D would say, "Everyone deserves a happy ending," and then she'd hurry us off to bed. Her husband, Papa, would yell at us to be quiet as we all ran down the hall and jumped in our beds awaiting our good night kisses. Sometimes Papa would join in but only if we didn't keep him up too late. Their home was always filled with laughter and the smell of fresh baked cookies. D's house was a safe haven for kids like us, kids without families or somewhere to go. The fact that it was cramped and there never seemed to be enough room, didn't bother us. What she gave us was a real home. Somewhere we could go and feel wanted, maybe even loved.

Many of us had the same story. Neglect and pain seemed to be a common lament as we would talk about our origins and the families we had encountered on our adventures. I myself had been tossed around from foster homes to girls' homes. I'm not exactly sure what they had against me, but it seemed I was never what they were looking for. With my brown hair and my eyes that were some drab color between brown and puke green, I wasn't the blond-haired blue-eyed angel most parents were envisioning. Momma D always took what they called, 'hard cases'. I guess that meant kids no one else wanted, like me.

I missed her house. I needed to call Momma D before we left and check in. I sighed as I turned back to my dishwater. There was still plenty to do before we left. I knew we would have to call the guys and make sure they were prepared for the long drive. Knowing Steve, it would take more than an alarm clock to get him up and going. Hopefully I can count on Damien to do the waking. A huge storm that had ripped through the town four months earlier hadn't even roused him, though hundreds were without power for days. With the dishes done, I walked down the hall toward my room; the only sound was the pit-pat of my feet on the hardwood. I flopped down on the bed and reached for the forgotten glass of milk on the end table. I took a big whiff and turned up my nose. Wrong glass. Maybe Sarah's right and I should try to be more organized. I looked around the room. Twenty years of my life and I still don't own any decent furniture, just a few picture frames with old photos of my bio mom and dad and an antique vanity that I saved from a yard sale. It sat neglected in the corner covered in make-up and clothes. I couldn't use the mirror because I had a collage of pictures all over it. I never enjoyed looking at myself anyway.

I'm starting to get closer to the age my mom was when she died. I could see her face more and more in mine, like her thin lips or the slight curve towards the end of her nose; the same petite features she had in her pictures. It's depressing really. Who wants to be reminded of their dead mother every morning? Besides my connection with the beyond in general, I didn't care much for the reminder. How does fate decide when our time is up anyway? Why was I left behind? Too many questions and not enough answers. That's why I had recently changed my major to Egyptian History. Maybe one day I would be a great historian in a museum, or an archaeologist, somewhere out in the desert. Maybe I could find peace there among the sand dunes and the ruins of once great pyramids. Big dreams that my parents could be proud of; maybe. I only hope they can look down at me and be glad with what I've done with my life. It would have been nice out of all the dead people I had seen come and go, if they had stopped by even once. I assume they had to be somewhere in the 'whatever comes after'.

The door swung open breaking my thoughts and there stood Damien, his shoulders completely filling the door frame. His hair was slicked back in a ponytail and the remaining dark strands sprayed along his face. He made an effort to tuck some of the strands behind his ear as his eyes twinkled down at me.

Such a cutie! I know my face was lit up because he gave me a sly smile and leaped on the bed beside me.

"Whatcha doin' here? It's a wonderful day outside to get some Vitamin D," he said in his motherly, mocking tone. I squinted my eyes and curled my nose at him.

"You know if you weren't so cute..." He kissed me before I could finish my sentence. This man made me so happy! I would follow him to hell and back if I had to. The rest of the morning we spent together, talking about places we would visit and things we would do once we got to Mississippi, while walking hand and hand through the park. It all felt like a dream, until he suggested stopping at every Hooter's along the way. I had to take a moment and give him the old 'girlfriend punch to the shoulder'.

"Hey! What? They have great wings there!" Now multiple swings were made and a few finger pokes to the ribs where I knew he was ticklish. Damien threw his arms up to protect himself. "Okay. Okay!" he said stifling a giggle. I stood on my tippy toes and kissed his cheek, by way of apology as he gingerly rubbed his pummeled shoulder, grinning. We had both been counting down the days to the most excellent adventure of our lives. Everything was looking up! If only we had known what was to come.

Chapter 3
THE SIGHTING

ONE day away from our greatest adventure ever! My insides felt like they were filled to the brim with butterflies causing my heart to feel fluttery. I'd never been anywhere outside the state but I did stay in a cabin once in the woods. That was one of the many trips Sarah and I had taken alone for a little girl time. We weren't built for roughing it so we rented a cabin. The two of us found a bond with the outdoors from within doors. We mostly watched chick flicks and did facials; you know the normal girlie stuff. I was just the normal amount of nervous. Who knows what we'll encounter? Still, being with my friends and the man I love on Spring Break; it's my idea of heaven. A little sun, some reasonable drinking, and long soaks in the hot tub awaited.

I was practically flying when Sarah and I left Damien and walked to our lecture hall building. Luckily, it was a wonderful spring day for the hike which made the journey more enjoyable. It was going to be hard to concentrate during the final in my English class, although writing is something I truly enjoy. I even have a little journal I keep by my bed in case I have a dream worth writing down, or sometimes I take it with me when I meditate after some Yoga. That's usually when I get my best ideas. The halls were crammed with students everywhere, reminding me of sardines tightly packed in a tin can. Sarah and I separated and headed to our different halls when I turned the corner and opened the classroom door. Looking around, I noticed that everyone actually showed up today. It's good to see that people are taking the finals more seriously than last year. This will be year two for me. After slipping into the room and finding a seat towards the back, I pulled out my spiral notebook for a quick review. The professor, Dr. Moore, continued discussing the differences in writing creatively and analytically writing. A fellow student was debating with her and she was doing her usual march back and forth displaying body language that said, '*Listen up, this is important*'! I'm sure she can't wait for the break either. What do college professors do on their vacations?

My mind wandered. I needed to focus and I mentally slapped myself. I've got to make a good grade on this exam to keep my scholarship. I tried shutting my brain off. Never works. I had allowed myself to get too wound-up about this trip. I still had another test to do before five. Thank goodness I studied the night before or I would be really bad off right now.

"Okay everyone, place your belongings under your seats and keep a well sharpened #2 pencil at hand. I need not remind you, this test is important and will greatly affect your overall grade." The exam had started and I didn't look up until I heard the bells from the clock tower indicating the hour was up. My neck was stiff and I rolled my head around gently trying to relieve it as I gathered my things. '*That seemed to go really fast*', I thought questioningly. We started to file out of the classroom looking like we had all just lost our puppies. Usually I spot Steve, Damien's brother, leaning against the display case waiting on Sarah, but it seemed they had gone on without me. Too bad Damien went to another school in the area. I continued to walk toward the psych hall.

It was unusually quiet in the halls even though it was the last day of classes. I wrapped my arms around myself, feeling cold, trying to keep the heat in. A little girl up ahead surprised me. She was out of place, wandering the hall with no parent around to care for her; far too young to be a college student. Dark stringy hair lay down over her face like a veil, it appeared wet and lifeless as it hit her shoulders. Her dress looked dirty and torn like she was in distress. I looked around to see if anyone else could see her too but the few people in the hall seemed to be moving quickly away from her. She just continued to stare at me, I could just make out her opened mouth. Something was definitely wrong here and I crept closer. My heart raced. It appeared that what I thought was a flowery dress was really dried blood spots! The girl reached her pale, long arms towards me in a gesture for help. I looked around once more hoping that someone else saw her too and I wasn't seeing another dead girl. Why am I always the one to notice? I looked back towards where the girl stood and to my surprise; she was close enough to me to touch. I almost let out a yelp and then thought better of it. Touching her was definitely the last thing on my mind, I recoiled trying not to look disgusted. The expression on the girl's half covered face only revealed that she was confused and frustrated, probably because I couldn't hear whatever she was saying. Her mouth opened and closed repeatedly but no sound came. She reminded me of a fish on dry land. The air seemed to drop even more in temperature as the girl started to flap her arms in a mad attempt to tell me something that appeared to be important.

Maybe she's just trying to scare me? What could be so important? She's dead and there's nothing *I* can do. I always feel like there is nothing I can do. I pushed myself loathing down. Seeing ghosts but not being able to help them was the dumbest super power ever. Did she want me to do something? I was now determined to find out what was so important. I placed my hands over my ears as a signal that I couldn't hear her. My head started to pound and I pinched the bridge of my nose to help the throbbing behind my eyes. A sudden voice in my head started laughing this cruel laugh making my headache turn into a violent throb. The laugh was deep and endless bouncing off the inside of my skull and making me feel dizzy. It sounded like a laugh that belonged to one of the bad guys in a James Bond flick; so cruel and relentless. The girl didn't seem to hear it. The kid in front of me was starting to blur in and out of focus as my head started to split wide from the pressure. The room swayed and the smell of honeysuckle was so strong, I had to cover my nose.

When I opened my eyes again, I was still in my English class. It appears I was frozen in mid-sentence. I look down at the paper to see what the last thing I wrote was. *'Don't go, stay at home,'* was written over and over. I broke out in a sweat and stared dumbfounded at the paper like it would come alive. The stanza repeated over and over in what appeared to be my handwriting. Was that what the kid was saying? I looked at the clock and could see that there were still 10 minutes left of class. The throbbing in my head was starting to dissipate as I looked around the room in amazement. What just happened? Did I just fall asleep? I didn't feel tired. I had so many questions but nowhere to get the answers! Confused and still a little dazed, I stood up to ask to be excused but thought better of it. No professor would let you leave in the middle of an exam but I couldn't take the staring eyes looking up at me any longer and headed toward the girls' restroom down the hall.

The room was small and felt safer than the open classroom. I walked over to the sink and splashed water on my face. "That was... different," is all I could think to say to my reflection as I reached for a paper towel. This has to be the first time in years that one of 'them' had tried to approach me in such a way. The bathroom door swung open breaking the silence, and in walked two giggling girls holding on to one another's arm, whispering frantically. All I wanted was time so I could think this out before I went crazy! I ran past the girls, who didn't protest, and rushed down the stairs toward the basement floor where there was another bathroom. One look around and I knew I was alone. A small stool was nestled in one corner and I gladly plopped down on it. Right now, I just didn't feel my legs could hold me. They felt like Jell-O, so wobbly and unstable. Why does this 'stuff' keep happening to me? 'They' always find the worst times to surprise me.

In the middle of an exam of all things! When I was younger, I remember talking and interacting with them, but age had taken its toll, and now they usually left me alone once they realized I was useless. Some kids had seen me talking to myself and rumors had started. They would come to me sometimes just to talk because they were lonely. I thought they were my imaginary friends; I was a weird kid. Their voices started fading out like someone had turned down the volume after puberty. By the time I was in eighth grade, I was starving for info. I had devoured every book in the library related to the subject of ghosts or cases where people had a gift similar to mine. Needless to say, most of it was in the fiction department. The internet became my best source of information once I reached high school. The only problem with that was credibility. How can you prove what you have seen if others can't see it too? That's my curse, which brings us back to the problem at hand.

The little girl really needed something to have continually tried to get me to understand what she wanted.

Maybe she wasn't around when charades were invented? That would have been a big help. Yep, I really needed this vacation. What about the warning? I glanced across the bathroom to take my mind away from the constant questions before it exploded. It wasn't the newest addition to the school but it wasn't peeling at the seams. I got up and went to one of the stall doors and nudged it open with the toe of my boot. The toilet seat was littered with cigarette burns from the smokers. Couldn't just wait to go outside, could you? I could hold it.

The clock tower rang loud over my head causing me to jump and I realized I still hadn't finished my test. I leapt back up the stairs two at a time and raced down the hall to the open classroom again with my heart pounding within its cage. I made quick dodges back to my seat to grab my things and make my apologies to Dr. Moore.

"I'm so sorry, Dr. Moore. I guess I was more nervous about this thing then I thought." I was holding my stomach to make her believe I'd been sick in the bathroom due to the extremities of her exam. My face was damp with sweat and probably looked pale too just to make it more believable.

"Well, I suppose I can come back early and allow you to retake the test before school reopens. When I saw you standing up, I thought you looked a little green and I did not need another vomit coated exam to be turned in today. Look, I see your hard work and I'm willing to give you a break just this once but please, let's keep this between just us. I have a reputation of being 'hard-ass' and I would like to keep it." She smiled at me and she could see the happiness in my eyes as they started to water. She knew I really wasn't a bad student! She patted me on the back on my way out. "Just don't make me wait."

"I won't, I definitely won't, I swear!" I followed her to her lecture desk as she picked up her calendar. We made our times and date while I continued to apologize. I had, to hurry I was going to be late for my next exam across the quad.

"Again, you're excellent, your class is amazing..." I rambled off backing up and bowing like an idiot. "If there's some kind of survey I could fill out for you, you'd get four stars, promise but I got to go!" I threw my thumb behind me as I stayed facing Dr. Moore, hoping for a head nod or something of approval. She waved her hand at me like she was swatting at a mosquito. That was the green flag I was looking for, so I turned and bolted down the hall. This time I saw Steve leaning against the far wall waiting for Sarah. He could see the relief on my face before I doubled over to catch my breath.

"You okay?" he asked obviously concerned.

"Never better," I replied holding a thumbs up that I could see swaying. I could feel my heart beating in my ears, and I needed a minute to calm my anxiety. I had promised Sarah I would walk across the quad with her before my next test, but due to recent events, I needed to get my head clear before that. "Hey, could you tell Sarah I'll catch up with her later? I really need to head on over and.... get a good seat."

"A good seat, for the exam?" he asked his forehead knitting up in the middle.

"Yah, it helps me." I started walking away so he wouldn't have more questions. "Tell her I'll see her at home!" I lightly jogged from him and to the double doors of freedom. The sun felt good on my face, but I had to squint for my eyes to adjust. What a day! I stopped at a bench in the quad, well away from the doors I had just escaped through. I retied my boots and straightened my shorts before collapsing onto it. Must get my head straight before the next test, which was in, I looked over at the clock tower, 15 minutes. I closed my eyes and focused on my breathing. '*Just focus on your breathing, don't think of anything else, you can do this!*' I thought. I closed my eyes. I took in the humming around me as students were going about their day. The feel of the sun's warmth on my skin. The breeze slightly moving my hair, silence in my head. I rolled my shoulders to loosen them and gently moved my head from side to side. Okay! I jumped up and bounced on the balls of my feet while shaking my hands at my sides. "I got this," I said to myself and walked the rest of the way with my face turned up looking confident.

The last test went quickly, I had no fingernails left but, I was free. I was using parts of my brain I didn't know could work to compensate for the other parts I was trying to keep off. I didn't feel much like patting myself on the back. What was done was done, right? Now I just had to walk across campus to get back to the apartment to pack. Sarah had been packing since we planned the trip a month ago, but I had studied instead. What good that did me. The studying I did couldn't prepare me for the surprises I kept getting at every corner. At least Dr. Moore had understood. I felt more confident about the retake I would have for her test than the one I had just finished.

I needed to get moving. Most of the students had cleared out so I didn't have to fake smile or wave at familiar faces as I made my way to our apartment. Opening the door with my key and stepping inside, I felt relief. I let out a sigh and flung my keys towards the bowl that held loose change. Almost made it in, oh well; I shrugged. I went straight to my room and flung my suitcases to the floor. A mixture of clean and dirty clothes lay beside them. Last minute packing is so easy! Why do people stress about it? '*Thank goodness for irons*', I thought looking at the wrinkled mess I was making. After forcing the cases closed, I stepped back and admired my work before proceeding down the hall to the kitchen. All this work had certainly built up my appetite. Sarah was already in the kitchen holding a sandwich out to me with a disapproving look on her face. She's so motherly.

"What?" I asked as I grabbed up the plate and turned to the breakfast bar to sit down.

"Steve said you were acting funny today before I showed up. Is there something wrong? Maybe between you and Damien?" she asked me with concern and a raised eyebrow. I knew Steve would say something, but I was hoping that Sarah's 'love for the dramatic' would hold out until tomorrow. She probably just assumed it had something to do with my relationship because we had spent the morning alone together. The real trouble, I wasn't ready to talk about yet, would have blown her hair back. So, thinking fast, I took a big bite of sandwich filling my mouth and buying me time to collect myself. My face is like an open book and if she gets a gander; the duck's out the pond (I know people say 'cat is out of the bag' but I think it's cruel to put it in the bag in the first place).

"No, nothing's wrong with Damien and me," I said around bites of bread and meat. "Besides, I wouldn't tell you. You would just run and tell Steve. You're such a gossip," I said, smiling to soften the sting as I removed mayo from the corner of my mouth. She knew I was teasing. When you've been sisters as long as we have...I'll leave the rest unsaid.

"Seriously? Steve said he was concerned." *Yeah right*, I thought. He has never been the type to worry about the welfare of others, besides the person he's dating. I guess I shouldn't think that about him, he is Damien's brother after all. I'm just very protective of Sarah. I would hate to see her in more pain than the world has already put her through. Her parents, or rather her mother, had left her on the doorstep of a sexually abusive uncle. Luckily, the neighbors became aware, and the state sent her to Mama D's. It took her a long time to trust men again. I just wasn't ready to accept Steve and I didn't believe he could ever live up to my standards. You must look out for your sister, otherwise who do you have?

"Well, he worries too much. No wonder you both are so great together." I put on a big smile through another mouth full of sandwich.

"You think so?" she asked with doubt in her voice and a tilt of her head. Changing the subject always helps, and it's even better when you make it about the other person. It was pleasant to just pass the evening talking about positive things instead of talking about what happened this morning. We went ahead with our late lupper and talked about our future with the guys. I avoided anything to do with ghosts or secret messages. She would most likely have me tell her everything, or at least, cancel our trip. Technically, we had already started our own little vacation with our feet up, jammies on, and soft mellow music in the background. Tests done, check. Bags packed, check. Just the boys to call to confirm our pick-up time.

"Don't forget to bring your trunks I bought you and sunscreen," I heard Sarah tell Steve over the phone. Such a worrywart she was. I left the room to give them some privacy and headed down the hall toward my room. Her voice faded as I closed my door and plopped myself down in the same spot I had been in that morning. Surveying the room, I noticed all the clutter had been shoved into two suitcases. My room looked clean at that moment. A distant voice yelled down the hall, "Jo, it's Damien!" I picked up the phone on the nightstand and put it to my ear but all I heard was static.

"Hello, hello!" I kept repeating into the receiver. It sounded like there was crying lightly in the background. "Steve, this isn't funny!" I said as anger started to rise in me. I was answered by a mixture of growls and screams through the static, it sounded like someone was saying something at a distance but was slowly coming closer. Almost like a train you can hear coming toward you. The voice gradually increased, growing louder by the second until I could make out the words, *"don't go, stay home!"* Over and over the words were repeated until it was so loud it sounded as though the other person was screaming into the phone. "Who is this?" I asked, but there was no answer, just the repeated warning. Oddly enough, it was the same warning I got earlier during my first exam. Why would someone want to stop me from going on this much needed vacation? What could be so important?

The continued paranormal warning broke my thoughts. The sound bounced off the walls and shook them until I thought the overhead light would fall and break. I put my hands over my ears and started to pray. I'm not a religious fanatic but I know where I come from. Only God could help me now. I can only hope he can forgive my transgressions and give me sanity. *'Please God please,'* I prayed, *'make the noises go away'.* The smell of honeysuckle hit me again and the vibration stopped. I slowly lifted my hands from my ears and looked at the phone for some giant hand to jump out, like at the end of 'Carrie' when the hand reaches up out of the grave. On the other end I could hear, "Jo, are you there? Hello, Sarah?" It was Damien's voice. I put the phone to my ear.

"Damien, is that you?" I asked, almost in a whisper.

"Well of course it is. Sarah told you I was waiting for you right?" I was shaking, making talking difficult. I cleared my throat and tried anyway.

"Yeah, she did, sorry. I guess I'm more tired than I thought."

"I just wanted to remind you I love you and I hope you have the sweetest dreams of me." He was being cute. It couldn't have been him that made that noise. Damien wouldn't do that to me. Did he hear it? Maybe Steve did it? There had to be a rational explanation, right?

"Don't forget about *Steve* in the morning," I said with an accusing tone.

"He's more excited than anyone I think." Damien responded, totally missing my cue. "As soon as he got off the phone with Sarah, he went straight to shower so he can get to bed early. You know, I think he's really in love with her. It's all he ever talks about. I've always wanted to see Steve as happy as I am with you." Now I felt bad. What a gushy sentiment that I *really* wasn't ready for after what just happened. How was I going to not ruin this moment for him?

"Only God can tell, and he's lost when it comes to Steve." Great, make a joke. Now is the time to mention I've got to wash my hair to get out of this. "You know, I really need to clean up a bit before I get ready for bed," I said in my sweetest 'don't worry' voice.

"Sure... no problem. I'll see you tomorrow bright and early. I love you." I could tell he was smiling on the other end. I am a convincing actress.

"I love you too, night," then click and there was silence. I slowly placed the phone back on the cradle and slid off the bed. My throat was dry but more than anything, I just wanted to get away from the possessed phone. I headed down the hall back to the kitchen. As I passed the bathroom, I could hear the water running. I guess Sarah beat me to the shower. I preceded into the kitchen and grabbed a cup from the cabinet. What had happened back in my room? Why had all this weird stuff started now? Was it because of the trip we were about to go on in the morning or something else, something more sinister? What could be trying to stop me?

God, I only wished there was someone to talk to about all this! Someone with actual answers. I grabbed both sides of my head in frustration. I wish I never had this. They say that people who have experienced a tragic event can end up with the ability to see things that others can't. I read that in some article on the internet. Tragic event, check; I made a check mark in the air with my free hand. I opened the fridge and found a soda can abandoned in the back.

Just think about the trip in the morning, I told myself. Ignore it and it will go away. I also read that the nasty spirits feed off the fear of those they haunt. The more you fear it, the stronger it gets. If you ignore it, it will dissipate. I took a sip of the soda and contemplated what to do. Maybe it was a warning? I laughed aloud; well obviously it was a warning! The thing I needed to figure out is what does it mean for me? Should I stay or should I go, as the old song goes.

I knew I wouldn't be able to sleep. Maybe some meditation would help me clear my mind. Regardless of the lateness, I retreated to the living room and grabbed my mat from the closet along with the journal that I had thrown in with it that morning. Yoga and meditation are my two favorite ways to relax and or decompress from the day. For one, no one bothers me, and second, I feel just like a normal person when I do it.

Fantasizing was good too. It was a chance for me to imagine myself somewhere else. I have the life I always wanted and I'm the head of some great museum. In other words, I could lie to myself and picture that I was just like everyone else with everyday problems. Sometimes when I meditated, I could see myself with my parents. We would be sitting back, relaxing and I would listen to them talk together. Other times, I could picture us on a worldly adventure trying to find lost artifacts of the Egyptians. I get lost in those moments completely and when I come out of it, I still think they're alive. Pretty sad, if you ask me, but now I needed to mull over everything that had happened over the last 24 hours. This could certainly take some time.

I began by placing the mat on the hardwood floor and tossed the journal beside it. After a few moments of stretching and some different Yoga stances, I sat in child pose and closed my eyes. Deep, soothing breaths in through the nose, out through mouth. I did this over and over while I tried to clear my mind. I don't want to say I was instantly taken to the happy place in my mind that I like to go, but it seemed like it was waiting, just towards the back to be discovered. I felt a tug pulling me along. Finally, the usual spot came to me, fresh and clear. I could almost hear the rushing water in front of me and the birds singing in the trees overhead. I, like always, am perched under a tree holding a book. I can feel the sun shining down on me making my skin feel warm and embraced. After glancing around, I noticed a couple sitting at the far end of the field laughing and cuddling under another tree. Normally, I don't see other people in the meditation, only in my dreams. Curious, I got up and walked toward them. Maybe this would be the answer I'm looking for. So many abnormal things have been happening that this didn't seem too out of the ordinary.

I was closer to the couple now and they should have noticed me, but they never looked up from one another. They were both frantically whispering. Occasionally a loud burst of laughter would erupt from the woman. I still couldn't make out their faces that were turned away from me. Now I was standing right next to the man, and I could hear my heart pounding in my ears. He was whispering something into the lady's ear and her head was down, giggling. I couldn't see either of their faces, but her hair was a beautiful shade of dark brown that shined in the sunlight. My hand grazed the man's shoulder, and he looked up at me with a smile. I was looking into my own eyes. Could it be? The woman glanced up at me and I could see her beautiful petite features in her delicate face and frame. I was looking at my parents? I was looking at my parents! There was more detail here then I could have gotten from any photograph. This time I wasn't dreaming them up, they were in my mind. That's the best way I can explain it. My imagination had never been able to make them look so real before! My mother reached her delicate arm up to me and lightly graced my elbow down to my hand where she held it. Both sat back a bit to get a better view of me. Dad stood up after what felt like ages, sized me up, then grabbed me in an embrace. Mother stood too with tears in her eyes, and she joined in the huddle. We were all smiling, hugging, and crying all together. It felt so good to finally be whole. I was imprisoned in their warm cuddle, and I let myself go. This is where I belonged. I was not alone anymore more.

*   *   *

The moment came when I found my voice and was able to ask questions about all this. Like she read my mind, Mom said, "He knows you have grown stronger, and he will continue unless you stop him. We all depend on you, my love." She stepped back to look me in the face better.

"Who are you talking about?", but then it came to me. "You mean the dark scary man from my dreams, don't you?" My eyes felt big with revelation.

"He has many forms but his reason for being is to create conflict and chaos upon the Earth," Father described, smile wiped now from his face.

"But what could he want with me and how am I stronger? I can't communicate with the dead...well until now." I indicated to them with a wave of one hand. That was the truth. How was it that I was standing here, with my dead parents, having a conversation, and all of it happening in my head? Did I stretch too hard and pop something in my brain? Was I dead? I pulled my hand through my hair.

"You have been blessed with a tremendous gift and you need to use it against '*him*'. You're getting stronger, even if you don't realize it. Just look around you! None of this could have been possible if not for you." She grabbed my hands and clasped them to her chest. "I wish we could help you further, but we can't interfere. *He'll* try to find you through us." Mother sighed, and it was beautiful.

"But we will always be around when you need us, kiddo," Dad finished. He pointed to his chest indicating his heart for further emphasis. That's where I had always kept them. I had so many questions, about life after death or if it hurts to die, but I could feel a tug pulling me back to reality. Dad and Mom were looking at me with such pride in their eyes holding one another. I only wished I could stay longer and get more info but seeing them for the first time in over twenty years, was enough to tide me over. Anymore may have been overwhelming and at least now I had some clue as to what had been going on.

"You must go, I feel him coming." She put her arms around herself like she was cold. The sky above seemed to get darker. I wasn't doing that. "Follow your instincts!" The wind started to pick up.

"Hurry!" Dad yelled so to be heard over the oncoming storm. I closed my eyes to fight back tears and when I opened them, I was sitting on the mat in the living room with the smell of honeysuckle all around me. The honeysuckle must have something to do with my parents! That explains one thing. My legs were sore and aching from being in the same position for so long. How long had I been sitting there?

Time flies when you're having a family reunion in your head. God, just thinking that makes me feel crazy. This whole ordeal is kind of out there. It's like I'm in some bad novel. My journal lay open next to me. I stood up and shook my legs trying to wake them. The clock in the living room was the only sound I could hear. It's almost one in the morning! I grabbed everything up in a hurry and threw it into the closet. Lord knew if Sarah saw this mess before we left, we would never get out of here. I also only had 5 hours of sleep to look forward to and my mind was racing. I needed to try and get some sleep. I hurried down the hall and saw Sarah's door cracked open. Well, at least the shower will be free. A warm shower should help me sleep. I grabbed some night clothes and headed to the bathroom.

The warm water ran over me and helped me to think more clearly. As I did my shower ritual, I thought about what my parents had said. I didn't even know where to start. Did my parents' tragic death have something to do with me? What's my purpose? Was I meant to die with them? The paper said it was a miracle I survived. They never found the trucker that hit us. Maybe if I could find him, I could find the answers. But what were the questions? Was the accident intentional? Did satanic voices tell you to do it like you see on those crime shows?

If the police couldn't find him, I doubted that I could. All I had to go on was the police report. Even with it, there was no description of the person driving or the type of vehicle involved. That's the problem when there's no witness. How would I explain some strangely random man hunt? Would I want to get my friends tangled in this mess? I rinsed my hair and decided that as long as I thought about these matters, the longer I would stay awake. I'd played Nancy Drew enough for one night. I needed to focus on getting some sleep before our big trip in a few hours. I turned off the water and grabbed a towel from the rack. The steam from the shower had fogged up the mirror. I wiped some of the moisture off it and found my face in the glass. It was red from the water and my hair was fluffy and stuck up in odd places. I began combing it back into shape, thinking about the fun we were going to have on the trip to keep negative thoughts and questions at bay.

Out of the corner of my eye, I saw a shadow behind me go across the mirror. No one could have come in behind me without me noticing. I turned around with a gasp, gripping my towel around me; no one there. I shrugged it off, it had been a weird day, what's one more thing. I brought the brush up to make another pass through my mangled mane. The lights in the bathroom started to flicker on and off drawing my attention to them. I looked back to the mirror, and almost fell over backwards. My heart raced. On the mirror, written through the steam, the words *'don't go, stay home.'* I ran from the room. Now I'd never get any sleep in my bed alone! Can't I just have a damn minute? I took a deep breath and blew it out slow, counting to 10. Then again. I stormed back into the bathroom and scooped up my clothes turning my nose up at the stupid mirror. I would have felt brave, but I ran out and down the hall to change into them.

I crept into Sarah's room and saw her sprawled over the bed, her hair still damp. I knew she wouldn't object to me sleeping next to her since that was often how we slept at the 'home.' I grabbed the edge of the cover and pushed her body over to make room for mine. I laid there for a while trying to quiet my mind so I could sleep. Every dancing shadow across the ceiling caught my attention. Overwhelming exhaustion took over my fear. Right before I drifted off, I had one last thought; what lay ahead of us in the morning?

Chapter Four
A NEW START
Frank

WHY did he have a phone in his hand? He didn't remember getting up to make a call and besides, who was he going to call anyway? As he stared at the receiver, he could hear a distant buzz mixed with white noise. He replaced the device back in its cradle and returned to the booth where he had been sitting. He nursed his coffee as he glanced wildly out the window.

Maybe something outside had prompted him to call someone? It felt like something was coming; maybe someone? Why couldn't he think? He rubbed his temples. Ruth, his regular waitress, tapped him on the shoulder to get his attention. He had to struggle to make his body respond before he was able to look up at her. She had her hair pulled back from her face in a bun and her apron already had a few dark stains trailing down the front. She indicated his coffee and he said, "Yes, thank you," in the politest way he could muster.

'Can't you do anything right,' the cruel voice in his head mocked him. The waitress was the only thing in his world that was a constant anymore. He knew every time he passed through town to stop at the diner, she would be there. She was *real*. Frank felt like a glacier being affected by Global Warming. Constantly changing, shifting slightly left or right, never to return to his original state; evaporating so slowly, you wouldn't even notice.

"Are you feelin' alright, Frank?" She looked down at him with concern while smacking her gum.

"Haven't been sleeping too well." He took his hat off and ran his fingers through what was left of his hair. "How's the family? Rob coming back from his tour soon?" He tried to smile up at her and it failed to be anything genuine.

"It'll be up in about 3 weeks, me and the kids are throwing him a welcome home party here if you'd like to come." Such a small town, here everyone made you feel welcome. How had he come upon this diner? He couldn't remember the beginning. He could only remember the voice; some crazy sound in his head telling him where to go, when to leave. Being a trucker and having no family of his own had been an advantage to him and his quest. Another reason why Ruth's party wouldn't be on his calendar.

"Sure, I'll check my route schedule to see when I'll be back," he lied replacing his hat on his head.

"Where ya headed this time?" she asked.

"Somewhere east, I think. Never sure. That's why I like the job so much." Really, the job was in North Carolina but he had planned on detouring to Tennessee because the voice told him there was someone there to meet. He nodded and smiled at the lady as she looked up and noticed another drifter with an empty cup. She was making him nervous with her questions. Soon he would leave and find another small town.

'Shut up! We must go, fool!' it hissed in his ear. He looked at his watch. He could be there sometime in the next day and a half. He didn't always hear voices. Well not plural-it was only one voice. He couldn't remember when it started, and he didn't know how it began. A drunken father and a dead mother could make a normal boy not so normal he supposed. He took one last

sip, appreciating the comfort in it. After tossing some change for the tip, he headed to the john. One little urinal, a busted toilet, and a sink with a mirror, made up the men's room. He pumped the soap dispenser and watched his reflection. His face looked like a stranger to him. Pale with sunken eyes, his clothes disarrayed and stained with oil and other fluids. What was he doing?

"Are you feeling sorry for yourself again?" his reflection asked with a smirk on its face.

"No," he replied sternly remembering how his father used to ask him the same question, which was usually followed by a beating. He wasn't going to let *his* boy grow-up thinking his life was any worse than anyone else's. He splashed some cold water on that smirk and dried it with a brown paper towel. Strange that replying to himself in the mirror had become so normal. He attempted to straighten himself up a bit before exiting the bathroom and making a beeline to the truck. It seemed like every face turned toward him as he left, making him even more paranoid.

The handle to his truck felt like a child's safety blanket under his hand. He instantly became relaxed behind his wheel, where no man could touch him. He took a few deep breaths of the warm stale air within the cab before he started her up. *'Okay, time to get it together,'* he thought as he put it in gear and started rolling away. Maybe this will be the last time and the voice would finally leave him in peace?

"Please God, let this be the last time," he said aloud. He wasn't sure if it was God or the voice laughing cruelly in his head, but he pointed his rig toward Mississippi and pulled out of reality, waving good-bye to his past life, and speeding to his destiny.

Chapter Five
HOTEL DREAD
Jo

I had only slept for a few hours, but it felt more like a few minutes. Sarah woke up to find me beside her. She was too busy to stop and ask why I was there, instead she leapt over me and made a dash for the bathroom. I was awakened by the bed being used like a diving board and I continued to lay there too excited to go back to sleep. Continuing not to think in the negative, I swung my legs over the side of the bed and rubbed the remainder of my dreams out of my eyes. My tummy roared with hunger, so I decided to skip the wait for the toilet and headed down the hall for some cereal instead. The smiling cartoon figure on the front should have helped with my optimism but I found his stare fake and vaguely creepy. By the time I was half finished, Sarah had come out of the bathroom looking thrilled.

She was wearing a bright pink tank top which went well with her dark hair and dangling earrings. You could see that she was wearing her bikini under it by the tie in the back. Sarah's figure was made for bikinis, and her long legs helped too. She also wore a pair of cutoff jeans and sneakers to complete the look. I envied her thin waistline, but Damien liked my curves, and that gave me confidence. She came into the kitchen and saw me looking her up and down. She modeled with a spin, and I applauded as she swung her hips to her auditory hallucination. We both giggled. This was already turning out to be a better day.

"What do you think? Too slutty?" she asked as she did another turn.

"Well, it's more, or should I say less, then what I was expecting." She pouted but came over to give me a hug anyway. My arms encircled her tiny waist easily.

"What are you planning on wearing?" she asked now taking a seat beside me. To think of it, I hadn't really thought about what I was going to wear. I had been a bit preoccupied with ghosts, insightful family reunions, and death threats on the mirror, so who could blame me?

"Does it really matter? We'll be in the car for most of the day anyway, and after a twelve-hour drive, I'll just change again for the beach." I looked up at her over the rim of my bowl as I slurped my milk.

"See that's where I'm ahead of you." She then pulled her bikini bottom partially out of her shorts to show she had the whole suit on under her clothes. She smiled at me and whirled around to the cabinet to get herself a bowl of cereal just as I wolfed down my last bite. I took my bowl to the sink and stopped to squeeze her cheek.

"You're so clever," I joked as I headed down the hall to my room to throw on my clothes. I guess I should have expected to feel rushed today. While I was throwing on my shorts and tank, I heard Sarah down the hall on the phone with the boys. The pressure was on, and I hurried to the edge of the bed where my flip flops and bags were waiting. I had to drag the heavy suitcases, which felt like dead weight, to the front door where they would later be placed in the trunk of Damien's car. I noticed Sarah getting off the phone and I looked up at her to make sure everything was alright. She was smiling so I'm sure Steve was the one that picked-up the phone. Good, that means he's up and we're even closer to getting out of here. Sarah grabbed her stuff and joined me at the front door. We waited on the porch like a couple of prom dates waiting for our princes to arrive. Sarah saw their jeep first, coming up our street, and I could feel the electricity in the air from all the excitement. Finally, we were getting this party started! We don't get out much, obviously. The guys exited our ride and came to the porch for our bags.

"You look excited." Damien said with a big smile on his face as he placed a soft kiss on my cheek. I followed him to the back of the jeep as he loaded in our things.

"I really need this vacation!" I replied. Most loaded statement of the year. He wrapped his arm around me in a half hug, as Steve and Sarah retreated to the back seat.

"Everything okay?" he asked closing the trunk.

"Nothing more than the usual crap." He looked me dead in the eyes like he was trying to read me and guess how serious things were. "Really, I'm fine, I would tell you if there was something to worry about." I put on a smile that felt more like a smirk and I could tell he wasn't convinced.

"As long as you promise to talk to me about it later, it can wait," he whispered as he leaned in and kissed my forehead. I gave him two thumbs up in the goofiest way possible as I backed up to take my seat in the jeep. I'm the queen of ruining a sweet moment. Damien smiled, then took his position behind the wheel as I took shotgun. The guys hadn't had breakfast yet, so we swung into a fast-food joint for some greasy biscuits, while Sarah and I just had coffee. The boys found my singing to be something to discuss as I turned up the radio that was playing my favorite song. They giggled and cracked jokes as we merged onto the interstate. Let's just say that I stopped after that despite their protests. There was a lightness in the car, a sense of normalcy. I felt the heavy pressure in my chest ease with each passing mile. There was no way some crazy death threat was going to ruin our trip!

We got to the Tennessee line in what seemed like no time at all. Amazing how thin traffic had been? Sarah and I complained about needing a potty break, so the boys pulled over at a rest stop. A visitor's center separated the men's rooms and the lady's room. The building was mostly colored in earth tones with a slightly slanted roof. There were a few people standing around, shaking the feeling back into their legs. Some were walking their dogs or their children around the park beside it. We split up to go to our respective bathrooms. The guys went quickly in but we were stopped short with a line. Why is there always a line at the girl's side but never at the boys? I guess we wash our hands. Thank goodness we weren't about to explode! The ladies up ahead were all talking loudly when I suddenly heard them mention the hotel we were to stay at that night. When the name came up, I immediately leaned forward to get within better range.

"Didn't ya hear, it's terrible...all those people.....don't know how...I heard it was a bomb..."

Sarah turned to me. "Did you hear that, Jo? My God, if we had come down any earlier, it could have been us," she whispered.

"That's weird, isn't it?" I reflected back to the message on the mirror. "Maybe they were talking about another place that just sounded similar?" My mind was racing. This couldn't be a coincidence, could it? Was it possible that someone was out to stop us? It seemed that whatever was going on, it was one step ahead of us.

"Well, when we get back to the car, we can check Steve's phone; see if there is anything on the internet about it. Still, you must admit, that's crazy!" Sarah almost seemed excited, but I knew her well enough to see she was panicking. All that planning sure didn't prepare her for this one! I had to be strong for her, I couldn't let my overthinking brain join in her panic.

"We'll tell the guys when we get back and see what they think. Don't let it bother you, Sarah." I patted her shoulder comfortingly. "Besides, maybe those gals had their info wrong?" She seemed to take that into consideration.

"We can find another hotel when we get there," she said slowly, "if it's even true." She paused and stared out into space for a minute. "I'm hope everyone is alright; those poor souls." I just couldn't think about that right now. I had to find some time to clear my head.

"I entrust, with it being Spring Break and all, we can still *find* another hotel. This sure is a way to start things off." She threw her hands to her sides like she was helpless, and I realized I wasn't helping. "We'll sleep in the car if we have to!" I added smiling to myself as I pictured the four of us all smashed into the car trying to sleep.

"That would be pretty funny," she responded, and we were both laughing again with some of the unpleasantness behind us. It was a relief once we got out of the bathrooms and back into the sunlight. The warmth against our skin made the endorphins kick in and off we ran to the car, to confirm the story.

After jumping in and buckling up, I proceeded to tell Damien and Steve what we had overheard in line. Steve didn't look too concerned as he looked it up on his phone, but Damien had his jaw set in a line which could only mean that he was in deep thought about something. I wanted to ask what it was but knew it would be better to wait until we were alone. Steve confirmed the story which was listed as being an accident. I was glad he didn't share the gory details, but we still needed to decide what we were doing next. Everyone was still psyched about continuing our trip, and we needed to look for a place to stop and eat soon anyway, so we agreed to come up with a plan then.

Steve and Sarah had been surprisingly positive about our predicament. They were smiling and had their arms around one another as we marched up to the restaurant. Damien and I hung back so we could talk a little before we went inside. "Damien, is everything alright?" I looked at him as he continued looking at the ground in deep thought.

"No, I'm fine, just got a lot on my mind." He reached for the door to the store. I placed my hand over his to stop him from going in after Sarah and Steve.

"I love you, and you can tell me anything...I promise. I just want to clear the air before we go in front of people." It felt weird to say, usually I was on the receiving end of that statement.

"I'm fine, there's nothing to worry about. We can talk later if you want." He put on a smile that didn't quite reach his eyes. It was still good enough for me for now and I smiled back. How could I be mad at him for not sharing when I had more than enough secrets I had yet shared? I'm not a hypocrite! In the back of my mind though, where a normal girl lived, I was wondering if Damien was mad at me in some way. Usually, when a guy looks upset, but he doesn't want to talk about it, it means it's about you. At least that had been my experience. I was hoping that girl was wrong, and I vowed to make time to talk to him about it later.

We had a pretty good meal considering the shoddy service. The TVs that were on showed displays of the wreckage that gave further testament to the stories we had heard about the hotel. Turns out that a gas leak had caused an explosion that left a lot of damage but, luckily, few deaths. Over lunch, we talked about our options and what we should do. After deliberating, we decided that we should keep on driving until we reached the beach in Mississippi. By then it would be around ten at night possibly. We knew that with it being Spring Break, there was a good chance that all the hotels would be booked. Our best shot would be to find a cancelation. How hard could it be, right? Sarah offered to make calls to the local and surrounding hotels to check on the availability and to feel useful. I say to feel more in control but that's just my opinion. With a plan underway, we jumped in the jeep and continued for the Gulf Coast.

The sights through Alabama were so beautiful that we didn't talk about anything else for the next billion miles. A few dark clouds had started to appear in the blue sky indicating that we were going to run into a storm sooner or later, but we didn't let any of that dampen our spirits. No pun intended. By the time we got towards the Gulf, it was dark and rainy. Sarah and I were chosen to go in and ask about vacancies. The rounds of calls to the locals she made had turned up nothing. Most of them said the '*first come, first serve*' rule was in play. I guess it's to be expected since it was the height of the season.

At the first few hotels we were hopeful, but everything had been booked in advance as expected and no one had called to cancel yet. After two hours or so, we were soaked and miserable, our hope held as we complained to the boys to look for the closest sign that said vacancy; not caring how the place looked. Damien went down odd streets that ran perpendicular to the beach. Trying for something off the beaten path. A small building with a bright pink neon sign came into view. The place looked like a dump from the outside, but the sign said vacancy. At this point we were only hoping to get warm and go to sleep as the clock ticked away to almost midnight.

After parking in the front, Damien and I went in. He wanted to make sure that the hotel wasn't full of crazies and rapists. My boy watches too much TV. We approached the desk, but it was empty, actually, the whole lobby was empty. Granted, it was late. There was a bell sitting on the desk beside a big black book that laid there exposed. I glanced at the book to look at the names and times people had come in and out that day out of curiosity. Damien went over to the bell and gave it a tap. The bell sounded dull like it was on its last ding. The lobby was a little shabby but there was a TV and what looked like a semi comfortable couch. The ceiling wasn't very high but there were tiles on it and the surrounding walls that appeared to be made of porcelain. Even with the lack of shine. There were a few plants scattered about that were still alive despite how terribly chilly it was inside. The air conditioner thermostat must have been broken on high. Fog covered the windows due to the warmth outside in contrast. Curtains hung thick with a shade of dark red that reminded me of blood over the main windows. The carpet appeared outdated and worn. It used to be this 60s style green shag, but it had flattened into a pea soup green with hardly any shag left in it. A family of spiders was nestled in the top corner and a few stuffed animal heads made the décor what it was.

Damien rang the bell again as he let out an exhausted sigh and out popped a small, stout, black man. He was unshaven and was wearing an open flannel shirt that still had a napkin tucked inside it. I guess we had caught him at dinner.

"Yeah, what'd ya want?" he said, wiping his mouth with the napkin while keeping it tucked in. What a hostel greeting!

"Just hoping that you might have a vacancy." Damien was stretching out his chest, trying to appear more intimidating, possibly.

"No, no room..." He said, disgruntled as he turned to go back behind a curtain beyond the desk.

"But your sign said vacancy." He indicated to the sign hanging outside. He paused to collect himself then said, "please sir, we're cold and tired. We'll be out of your hair first thing in the morning, I promise." I was tired and desperate to get into some dry clothes but even I was having second guesses about this place. I tried to smile at the man, but it didn't break through and shine like I wanted it to. I was just too tired.

"You'll be out in the mornin', eh? Well maybe she won't mind...oh, but you best sign in." He pushed the book toward us and departed behind the curtain to retrieve the keys. I stood beside Damien as we both just looked at each other and shook our heads. Who knew what the guy was on about. We signed our names in the dusty book just as Steve and Sarah came in through the door behind us. They must have gotten tired of sitting in the car waiting.

"What's taking you guys so long? I thought there might be trouble." Sarah had her body completely pressed up against Steve's back, probably scared to death at the thought of being in here. Did I mention we didn't get out much? This place made all the hairs on the back of your neck stand up so I couldn't blame anyone for feeling things were off. It did kind of remind me of the movie *Psycho* with the stuffed heads and the creepy host and all.

"We just had some trouble with the bell and..." Damien was cut off by the sounds of the man coming back to distribute our keys.

"Here ya all go...oh, there's more of you." He looked up and down at the other pair questionably.

"We really are thankful for this, sir. What do we owe you?" I asked putting his attention back to me.

"I'll take one fifty from you now please." He had his hand outstretched toward Damien. I thought for a moment that my fiancé would try to haggle with the man seeing as the room would only serve a purpose to us for a few hours and we had brought a limited supply of folding money. Maybe it was because *I* didn't like paying full price if I didn't have to. The place was more a motel then hotel since it was one floor and looked so out of date that I knew there would be no credit card machine we could use. Probably no room service either. Damien reached down into his pocket and pulled out a handful of 20's.

After paying the man and happily returning to the car for our belongings, we walked around the building to our room. It appeared to be the last room open on the bottom floor. A few motorcycles lined the parking lot along with a lot of pick-up trucks. It gave the place the feeling of danger but I knew not to judge a book, or building, by its cover. In the distance I thought I heard someone scream, but it was only a cat I saw as it leaped across the lot. Still, Sarah and I stayed close together as the boys circled around us until we opened our motel door. What had we gotten ourselves into?

Chapter Six

GIANT SPIDERS AND SCARY STUFF (OH MY)

AFTER getting to the room, we remembered why we got it so cheap. The wallpaper had small, faded pink flowers on it and was peeling down the middle. Straight ahead was the bathroom which didn't look inviting at all. It was very cold in the room, and the machine appeared to be busted. Sarah and I took turns in the bathroom changing into some dry clothes. We decided that we would sleep on top of the sheets, despite the cold temperature, which is also why a change of clothes was appropriate. The sheets had a funny smell like they hadn't been changed in months so sleeping on them rather than under sounded like a good idea. It was just for the night anyway, no need to be too fancy. The room wasn't inviting at all, but it was at least dry. We were finally out of the rain and close enough to the beach to smell the salt water.

Steve called the bathroom next, which allowed Damien and I to call on bed preferences. It was a tossup between a queen with a stained comforter or a pull-out couch. We totally took the bed. Sarah joined Steve to finish up her evening ritual of brushing her teeth and removing old runny make-up. Since Damien and I were alone for another moment, I took the opportunity to recap on the questions I tried to ask him earlier.

"So, do you want to tell me what's wrong besides the obvious?" I sdked, indicating the room for flare.

"It's just...I don't know, you'll think I'm crazy." His eyes went to the floor as I sat beside him on the bed.

"I think I'm the leading authority on crazy here and my determination is," I poked his forehead for dramatic effect, "not crazy. Besides, we all go a little crazy sometimes." I put on my best Jack Nicholson eyebrow move. He laughed; I love his laugh. It was like a sweet song that could coax the angels down from heaven.

"I love you. You always know what to say to make me feel more normal." Normal? How could I make anyone feel normal? My thoughts were interrupted by a loud shriek coming from the bathroom followed by a thump. Damien and I both jumped and turned towards the bathroom. Steve swung the door open, and Sarah flew past him.

"What's wrong, Sarah?" I said as I hurried over to her. She was shaking violently. Steve was the next to come out of the bathroom but with a smirk on his face.

"Man, what the hell was that!" Damien asked as I stroked Sarah's shivering shoulders.

"It was just a spider, man. It was a real ugly one, though, went down the drain before I could squish it." He wiped the toothpaste from his mouth with the back of his hand, smiling the whole time. I frowned at him. Sarah has arachnophobia and it was nothing to smile about.

"Oh my God, that was the biggest, hairiest spider I have ever seen! If there are more of those around, I don't think I can sleep here." She was holding herself to keep from shaking apart. Steve walked over to her and put his strong arms around her shaking ones. I squirmed out of the big hug and let him take over the comforting.

"Come on babe. It's just for tonight, then we'll be traveling down the coast looking for something better to be open, far away from here, okay?" Steve seemed optimistic but this whole thing was already starting to look gloomy. I hoped something good was about to happen to save this trip.

"I think I'd rather sleep in the car. Do we really have to stay here?" She looked up at Steve, craning her graceful neck around to show him her face, full of fear and emotion.

"Look, I'm sorry. I thought for sure there would be more hotels with cancellations than this. We can't go back after coming all this way! Just one night, baby. Don't look at me like that." She was pouting at him now, knowing he hadn't been the one who put a big spider in this awful room. That he hadn't caused the explosion that blew up the hotel trapping us here, but feeling as she did, the look was deserved anyway. It was sweet that he was trying to comfort her, anyway.

'Sure, we could give this trip a second chance after tomorrow; a new start. This was just a fun story to tell,' I thought. The crazy, stinky hotel room covered in spiders, or at least that would be her side of it.

"Look I'll check the couch before we go to sleep, okay. Make sure it's all safe for my little cupcake." She really frowned then but she couldn't hold it. She went right into a big, beautiful smile. The poor girl really loved him to stay the night in a place like this after what just happened. At least everyone was smiling again.

"I'm sorry I acted so foolish just then. I don't know why I let those creepy crawlers bother me so much!" I could see the pulse in her neck had finally slowed down. Before, it was pounding so hard, you could see it across the room.

"It's no problem really," Damien and I both said in unison trying to look anywhere else in the room to keep her from embarrassment. We both knew she was terrified of spiders. That and not being what she calls 'properly organized'; drives her crazy. Kind of like me and ghosts.

"I think we could all use a drink, after that," Steve said as he released Sarah and walked towards the cooler we had packed that morning. "Beer or Diet, man?" he motioned towards his brother.

"Diet," he said in reply as he reached towards the outstretched can.

"You're such a pussy, dude," Steve whispered to his brother as he shook his head and opened the cold beer in his hand. "Diet for the ladies too, I imagine."

"I'll take a beer," Sarah squeaked, surprising us all. Must have thought it would help calm her down. I grabbed the diet and took a seat on the edge of the bed. The soda felt cool and refreshing against my parched throat. Sarah chugged her beer hungrily before she crushed the can in her fist to show she was finished.

Steve was already reaching for another as the rain continued to beat on the roof overhead.

*   *   *

The alarm clock on the nightstand beside the bed blinked three a.m. A noise had awakened me. In the stillness, all I could hear was snoring coming from the guys and a slight mumble from Sarah across the room. What woke me up then? I opened my eyes fully and peered around. The bathroom light was on? But I could have sworn we had turned it off. Sarah probably got up and turned it on because she was scared. Maybe that was what woke me? I got up to turn off the light but had to open the bathroom door the rest of the way to do so. The tub was full of soapy water. Who would take a bath and forget to drain the water?

I reached my hand towards the suds in hope of finding the plug and draining the fluid. Like something had sensed me coming, the water under my hand started to shift and move. Slowly, a head emerged, all wet and matted down, dark in color. The hair was long and landed on slim bare shoulders as they came up from under the liquid. I was frozen in shock and fear as a naked girl became visible from the depths. Her face started to turn upwards to me and I turned away, afraid to look into those dead eyes. Unfortunately, I was now facing the bathroom mirror and I was able to get a full view of the going-on behind me.

I stared open-mouthed at my own reflection as the woman fully emerged from the water. Her face now down; her hair hanging wet and plastered to her head. Her body was all pale and she was bending slightly over where she stood. Did I mention she was naked? I could feel the heat rising in my face as I attempted to calmly leave her in peace. I had to get everyone out of this horrible place! We'll stay in the car like we had suggested earlier. Anything but in this place for one more minute! I could feel her shoot waves of loneliness and pain into my body. I almost doubled over from it and had to grab the door for support. She threw the door away from me and it met the frame with a hard smack. Okay, this was new. I went immediately and tried to open it, but it was stuck. How was I going to get out of here?

I banged on the door yelling, "Hey, guys, I'm stuck in the bathroom. Hello? Somebody, wake up!" Still no answer. I heard the girl behind me getting out of the tub and start across the floor towards me. Panic rose as I imagined being trapped in the room with what felt like a really pissed off ghost. I banged even harder on the door and tried shaking it free from its frame. A sudden loud scream from the other side stopped me in my efforts. Loud voices followed and I thought maybe they heard me, and I would be free of this nightmare. I could feel the girl's cold presence up and down my back as she crowded against me. Why hadn't they opened the door yet? Loud muffled voices on the other side continued. What was going on out there?

What if the same thing that was going on in here was going on out there? They needed my help! I felt the girl's icy hand on my shoulder and I put all I had into pulling the door open. A charge flowed through me as my hands tingled like they had gone to sleep. A brilliant light grew from them and hit the door with such force that it splintered into a thousand different directions. The force knocked the girl away from me and I stumbled forward through what was left of the opening. I glanced back and saw the girl lying on the floor looking up at me with a shocked look on her face. I tried not to look as shocked, so instead I smiled. Sure, I did that on purpose, just you watch out; I'm not your average girl! I had no time to waste, my friends were in trouble, so I swiftly jumped around the debris to see what was going on. The scene before me was one I will never forget.

Damien was reaching out to Steve and Sarah but the sheets had turned into snake like tentacles and had coiled around him so tightly he couldn't get free. Steve's hair was alive with maggots which were falling off his head and hitting his shoulders as he tried to help Sarah squish all the spiders that were coming after her. Steve's pillow on the couch bed moved upward with more of the disgusting insects underneath. That explained one thing but that wasn't even the worst part. The worst sight was Sarah's abusive uncle standing in the middle of the room with spiders spitting out of his mouth every time he opened it. Each of them varied in size with dark hairy legs and small bodies. They scrambled quickly down the front of his shirt to the floor like a wave. A gargle of words came out of the man that sounded like, "harlot... shacked up... boy!" When he said boy, a huge amount came tumbling out. They were all running up to Sarah who was swinging a large boot wildly and crying. Steve operated the other boot, squashing or shewing away the survivor. She was pleading with the man that looked like her uncle. To make matters worse, I could hear the girl behind me start to get up. What should I do? How could I help? My body trembled with fear and the chill from the room as my breath came out in short puffs of cloud.

I reached out to Damien who was closest, and tried to beat the sheets off him, only to hit him instead. "Grab my pocketknife off the dresser, Jo. Hurry!" I grabbed the knife, and I took a deep breath. I didn't want to stab the man I loved but I didn't trust my hands that were now shaking. I had to be very careful not to hit him. I pushed my will and what was left of my energy down into the blade. I sensed the same sensation in my hands as I had in the bathroom. When the blade hit the sheets, it ripped through them with a bright light. The sheets exploded leaving pieces of fabric slowly drifting down around us like confetti. No time to think about it, Damien was free and now to help Steve and Sarah. Whatever I was doing seemed to work and that was all that mattered.

Damien didn't hesitate, he ran to the ghostly abuser and grabbed him from behind. He grunted as he squeezed the specter, lifting him off the ground, then sent him flying into the corner away from the others. A black aura materialized around the attacker as he attempted to stand back up. The spiders stopped for the moment and Sarah was able to get to the door that she had been trying to reach since this all began. She pulled it open with ease and the fresh air flooded the room. I looked back where the man had landed to ensure that he wouldn't be running after her, but he was gone. Sneaking a peek back towards the bathroom, I noticed the girl was gone too. My head was spinning with questions, and I felt lightheaded. Steve went to join Sarah outside as Damien came over to me and placed a supportive arm around my waist. We took a moment of silence and placed our foreheads together as we caught our breaths. We then emerged from the room, looking over our shoulders just in case.

"What the hell was that?" Steve yelled over Sarah's head as she remained cradled in his arms.

"Is he going to come back for us?" Sarah's voice was muffled but you could still hear the rattle in it.

"Let's all just calm down guys and get our heads together." Damien reassured us. I was glad he was taking control of the situation because my head still felt fuzzy.

"Calm down! We were just attacked by God knows what and you want me to calm down? I say we torch that room. Those SOBs can't get away with that!" Steve yelled in frustration while pumping his arm back towards the open motel door. He looked down at Sarah and stroked her face. She still looked terrified. Did he realize that they were ghosts? Probably poltergeists if I'm being honest. First ones I had ever encountered and hopefully the last.

This is all my fault. Maybe it was a warning and not a threat I kept seeing? We should have stayed at home! I felt like crying but I was too tired, even for that. I guess blowing that door up had taken more out of me then I had realized. All my adrenaline was gone, and I felt weak. How did I do that anyhow? My questions were interrupted by Sarah's whimpers.

"He was so cruel to me. How did he find me here?" She was delusional and actually believed the man in the room was her uncle. There's no way he was; just a ghost who knew her weakness and played on it. Poor Sarah wept into Steve's broad chest.

"It's okay, Sarah." He stroked her hair. "That wasn't really your uncle, babe. That man will never hurt you again as long as I live." He kissed the top of her head and rubbed her back slowly.

With Sarah being taken care of, I turned my attention to Damien. He was staring down at his hands with a look of concentration on his face. He saw me looking and he quickly dropped his hands to his sides; rubbing them on his pants like they were dirty.

"You okay?" He asked me. "We didn't know where you were during all the commotion."

"I was trapped in the bathroom with a naked ghost girl." The words came out sounding more hate full then I wanted but I felt like he was hiding something from me and he kept avoiding talking about it.

"I'm going to kill that manager for putting us up in a place like that!" Steve was trying to turn towards the office where we had signed in but Sarah held him tight and wouldn't allow him to move. "Come on honey, I'm going to kill that manager for what he did to you. At least give him a piece of our minds. Come on Damien!" He motioned with his head towards his brother.

"Now Steve, maybe he didn't know, man." Damien started holding his arms out in a "slow down" gesture.

"Well, we should definitely go up there and tell him about his little problem then! Come on Damien, I figured you would be with me on this one, bro." We all looked at Damien, even Sarah.

"Fine then, let's go wake this f'er up then!" That put a smile on his brother's face. I took over holding Sarah as we trailed behind the boys marching up to the office. The parking lot was eerie quite as we approached the door. The sign hanging on it now said closed but it was unlocked so we took the invitation and walked right in. Nothing like a nightmare to get your courage up! Damien went straight up to the desk and started beating on the bell repeatedly. Steve joined him at the desk while we gals hung back in case a quick exit was warranted. It probably took a good ten minutes before the manager came from behind his curtain.

"Hey now, stop that," the man started, then he had a look of recognition on his face, "oh, it's you folks again." He tried to straighten up the crooked shirt that he had apparently just put on. We must have woken him up. There must be a bed back there somewhere.

"Yeah, it's us you bum! You rented us a haunted room that tried to kill us!" Damien said while slamming his fist on the desk.

"Look kids, I didn't think she would mind, okay? You wanted a room and that's what I gave you." He tried backing away from us, but Steve stepped closer to him with his finger pointed at the other man's chest.

"We wanted a room to sleep in not be terrorized in! You got some kind of sick problem giving anyone that room!" He was practically screaming at the man as he poked him with every other word he said. I can't believe he knew and would put us in there. Those two in the room were trying to scare us to death! What if someone got hurt? Wait!?

"You said you thought 'she' wouldn't mind. There was a man and a woman that both attacked us. Do you know what or who they are?" I asked curious he only mentioned one.

"Listen kids, it's been a long night." He had his hands up looking like he was innocent. "How about we have story time at a decent hour," he smiled showing rows of dingy teeth.

"How about I break your face," Steve said taking his outstretched hand and turning it into a fist.

"Now there ain't no need for violence, my friend." He cowered behind his hands.

"We're not your friends! Maybe I should let my brother here show you some manners. Or, how about we call the police? Maybe that would help." Damien threatened at the manager.

"No need in doing that. I was just trying to help you all out," the manager whimpered. Like he did us any favors!

"Help us out by telling us what the hell is going on here. I was just attacked by a man that looked like my uncle, but he was spitting spiders everywhere. It was awful!" Sarah spoke up for the first time since we were outside. I looked down at her and thought how brave she had been through this whole thing. It's one thing when I see ghosts, but when they start bothering my friends, we have a problem.

"I'm sorry little lady, I didn't mean for no harm. I'll even give you a partial refund in light of the situation." The manager placed his hand over his heart as a sympathetic gesture.

"You're damn right you're going to give us a refund. A full one! What are you? Demented?" Steve yelled at him.

"Now there's no need for name callin', folks. I want to help. Look, there was a murder a while back and a woman died in that room. I don't know nothing about no guy. Maybe you were mistaken?" Anger boiled in me, the nerve of this guy! I sensed Sarah's body tensing beside me.

"This isn't a good time to call us a liar, sir. There certainly was a man and we'll prove it!" Sarah grabbed my hand, turned around, and headed for the door. Everyone else had been brave for her, but Sarah was no lying coward. I could hear them moving behind us and I knew they were following. Good, now let's get back to this room and get things sorted out. Let this sicko see what we had to deal with.

As we reached the lobby door, the handle turned in front of us, opened by a heavy-set woman in large robes of some kind. Now what?

Chapter 7
NEVER TAKE CANDY FROM STRANGERS

SARAH held the door as the woman in heavy robes limped in past me and turned around to get a better view of us all. "Am I too late?" she asked, looking concerned.

"Too late to get a room, madam. I am sorry but come back in the mornin' and I think I'll have something by then." The manager looked her over and bounced his eyebrows. There was nothing redeemable about this guy. I noticed her upturned face as she brought it into my general direction. She had high cheek bones and rosy cheeks. She wore no make-up, but she looked like she never needed any at all. Her skin tone was very complimentary to her hair which was the color of hay with light showings of grey, all pulled back in a neat bun. She should have been at home baking cookies for her grandchild instead of here in this mess.

"Oh no, silly, not a room." She chuckled at the manager. "My dear, you look shaken up." Her face showed worry as she walked over to Sarah and started digging in her oversized bag. "Here child, chew on this. It will make you feel loads better after a bit of a fright." She handed Sarah what looked like liquorice with a grin, and Sarah looked at it questionably. "Don't worry child, I dabble in homeopathy. I find that herbs and roots make you feel better quicker than those awful drugs they advertise."

Sarah still didn't seem convinced. "This is a dried bamboo root that has calming qualities. It doesn't taste half bad either."

Sarah put a little in her mouth and slowly sucked on it to get the lady to hush. I looked over at her and gave her a reassuring glance. Normally older people carried around hard candy but if it worked, it worked. What an odd stranger.

"I'm sorry lady but we got to get back to our room. Thanks for the root and all," Steve said as he grabbed Sarah's arm and ushered her outside. She *was* starting to perk up a bit.

"Yes, let's go back to your room. There's a problem there I would like to address," she added, shrouded in mystery.

"Wait, you know about the room?" Damien asked suspiciously.

"Of course, why else would I be here at four o'clock in the morning? I knew all about this before you all even got here. I just got caught up and didn't arrive in enough time to warn you." She gave me the hairy eyeball.

"What are you, some kind of psychic or something? This place is crazy. They got crazies coming out of the woodwork." This from Steve.

"I would prefer a bit more respect than that, thank you. I work in things that most don't believe in. You would be surprised at the things I know about you right now. I want to discuss this further, but we only have a few hours or so before daylight. After that, we would have to wait until tomorrow. You can only do these things at the time they died." She gripped her robes in one hand while holding her bag in the other as she started off towards our motel room. Over her shoulder she said, "I was caught up at the library researching the article about their deaths."

"So you uncovered the *two* deaths here?" I was now fully invested and felt rejuvenated with a new sense of direction. "We saw a man and a woman, but they didn't seem to acknowledge one another. I thought they would gang up on us but thankfully they didn't." Why was this lady so easy to talk to? I walked faster till I was in step with her.

"The dead can't see each other, that's why they're so lonely, poor dears. They have only the living to interact with. In this particular case, the woman and the man are husband and wife, and both died in that room. Now please, all will be revealed but for now we must hurry!"

"We? Look nice lady, we just left that hell hole. I don't know what is going on; I'm not about to let my friends go back in there with you. It's far too dangerous and you look like a professional. We'll wait outside for you if you want, with an ambulance." Damien looked at her, totally serious about every word he said.

"Damien, I need your power and Josephine's to stop them both." She turned and faced us. "I don't have enough strength left for the two of them. I need your help. I will assist you, guide you through your powers. But you must trust everything I say and do exactly what I tell you." She dug through her bag once more and I could just make out what she was saying with her head down. "We have little time, children, and I will tell you what I can afterward." She turned back towards the open door just a few more steps out of reach. How did she know about me? What power did Damien have that she needed? I looked to my friends for the answers, but they all just shrugged.

"Are you coming?" I asked Damien giving him a chance out.

"I'm not letting you go back in there alone," he replied. I smiled and reached out my hand to him. He grasped it and joined me at the threshold of the room. This was turning out to be some crazy vacation.

Chapter Eight
GOOD DOG
Frank

HOW did that hag know where we were? Frank crawled into a men's room at the rest stop. He dragged himself over to the sink and pulled himself up to let the cool water run over his bloody hands. He glared up at his reflection. Blood trickled down from a slash across his forehead and one of his eyes was black with bruising. Gingerly, he touched the scratch and cringed a bit. *'Straighten up, we can't let her get away!'* yelled the voice from within.

"I can barely stand, okay? What more do you want from me!" he yelled at his reflection.

"You should have killed her. You were weak!" his reflection yelled back at him. He took more water and splashed it on his face.

"She was too powerful for me! Why don't you come out and fight her instead of leaving it to a fragile body like mine. You think you're so powerful." The voice raged through his brain, giving him an intense headache that made him grab both sides of his head.

"You're a pathetic member of your race! I should just kill you now but we have to get to Mississippi before her," the voice hissed. The witch was probably already there by now. He tried to hold her off, but she had strength and magic on her side. How could he have a chance? "I think I'm going to have to call for some assistance if you cannot do this alone," the voice told him.

"Who would want to help us?" asked Frank.

"Oh, you shall see," said the cruel voice followed by an evil laugh. Frank didn't like the sound of that. It's bad enough to have an old witch after you but to be traveling in search of a girl you're going to kill; this was madness. What could be in store for poor Frank now? The trucker washed off the blood and tried to stand on his own without the sink. He was still wobbly, but he could walk as he felt tenderly at his side. She had slashed him with something invisible and now a gash remained. There were also various slashes across his arms. They had all been made by the same invisible blade. That stupid witch!

The next time Frank saw her he was going to make sure she got her comeuppance. He angrily grabbed wads of paper towels and pressed them over the wounds. By the time he was ready to leave the bathroom, the sink, floor, and mirror had blood on it. He cleaned up as best he could and placed the soiled rags in the garbage as he left. The fresh air outside helped him relax a bit more as he limped to his truck. When he got to his rig, he almost fell over. "She popped my tires, that skank!" he screamed into the night.

"No matter, help has arrived," the voice hissed into his ear. A growl made Frank turn around quick. Standing close to the vehicle was a big, black dog. This was no normal dog. Its head easily came up to Frank's chest. It had glowing ember eyes and it foamed at the mouth. Oh, and it could speak.

"I am here master," the mutt snarled. "What will you have of me?" It bowed its giant head towards the ground.

"Let's fix these tires and be on our way," Frank's mouth moved in response but it was the voice controlling it. What was this creature? The dog went right over to the tires and examined them, turning its head side to side. After pacing back and forth in front of the tires, the dog latched on to one like it was going to gabble it down.

"No!" Frank cried thinking about his truck and how much he cherished it.

"Shut up fool. Look." The voice hissed at him. Sure enough, when the dog bit into the tire, it actually filled up with air. The animal went around to all eight wheels that had been deflated and repaired them. Afterward, the dog came back up to Frank awaiting more orders.

"Good dog," Frank stated it like a question as he reached his hand towards the beast.

"Don't touch him! He is no mere pet," barked the voice in his head. "Now my servant, you are to come and help us to defeat that old witch." Frank's mouth moved again on its own. Was he supposed to ride with this beast? His legs felt like jelly as he took a minute to think of how that would look. '*To the truck, you idiot. We must hurry!*' the voice commanded in his head. He hadn't questioned anything the voice had told him so far, so he scrambled over to the cab and opened her up. He allowed the dog to climb in first and be his co-pilot. Maybe this trip won't be so lonely with company along, he thought. But who would want company with a hell hound or a hideous voice? Only Frank Holtz. He felt more confident with his new companion. The two started off on their journey, not knowing what it would hold for them, but they did know that someone was going to die.

Chapter Nine

FOR THOSE THAT DON'T LIKE VIOLENCE, LOOK AWAY!
Jo

THE old lady limped and dragged her feet, but we were in no hurry, nor did we want to go in first. The office manager had caught up to us partially out of curiosity but mostly to ensure that we didn't do anything to his precious room; totally overlooking the fact that his room had almost killed us. Damien looked at his watch and shook his head; we didn't have much time left. It would be daylight very soon. Not like I have a clue as to what we are about to do anyway. I could only hope this lady knew what she was doing. At least afterward she had promised to give us the answers to our questions. That was the best incentive to follow her, not that a cleansing of the room wouldn't be cool to watch.

The door was still ajar from our hasty exit. The lady went right up to it and bravely stuck her head inside. "Well, it looks like they have receded back into the room," she yelled over her shoulder. "Damien, Jo; I need you both to come over here and take my hand." Damien and I traded glances behind her back and then reluctantly went to either side of her. Hesitantly we both reached down and grasped onto her cold hands. I wasn't ready to go back in yet and the expression on Damien's face reflected mine. What would be in store for the three of us once we went in?

"Jo, please don't go back in that place," Sarah cried out from behind us.

"I'm telling you all, there ain't nothing wrong with my rooms!" yelled the office manager, planting his balled-up fists on his bony hips and watching for other potential customers. I'm sure this scene wasn't the only thing *bad* for business.

"We'll be okay Sarah, I promise." I tried to give her a reassuring look over my shoulder, but I knew it failed. Honestly, I didn't know what we were walking into and the pit in my stomach was growing. We had just run from this room not even an hour ago and then magically, this lady had shown up and talked us into walking right back into hell. She didn't even have to bribe us with candy, just the lure of knowing ourselves better, which, I know, sounds crazy.

I felt a tug on my hand which meant it was time to head into the room. The lights had been turned on and I squinted against the glare as I entered from the darkness outside. It appeared normal, nothing was out of place. It was almost like we dreamt the whole event but how could we have all had the same bad dream?

The old lady broke the silence. "Okay kids, I'm going to need you to listen very carefully to everything I say no matter how ridiculous it might sound at the time."

"I think it's pretty ridiculous that we're here right now, so fire away. I don't think anything could surprise me at this point." Damien shot quick glances around the room.

"Even so…" She let go of our hands and reached into her bag that was hanging limp at her side." This is for you, Josephine." She handed me a small knife.

"What am I supposed to do with this?" I looked at the item in disgust. "They're already dead. It's not like I can kill them again!" Maybe putting our fate in this old bag hadn't been such a good idea.

"Honey, with your skills, I thought you'd be a bit more open-minded," she sighed. "One of your talents is the ability to put energy into items to make them effect supernatural beings." She could see that I didn't understand, and I started to shake my head at her in confirmation. "When you cut Damien free of the blankets that held him down like evil snakes, didn't you notice a bright light coming from the weapon that you held? You put your power into the blade. You'll find you can do this with almost any object and eventually, you'll evolve past the need for physical items to project through." I had a bewildered expression on my face. How did she know? Had she been spying on us? She continued like she didn't notice. "The door you exploded, that will happen until you can control yourself." I turned the knife over in my hand, but my mouth stayed slack and open with disbelief. "Don't look so worried, you will do fine." She patted me on the shoulder as I stood gazing down at the blade.

Damien stood poised by the lady with the bag like the Cowardly Lion looking for his courage medallion. "I didn't forget you." She smiled up at him while reaching into her bag.

"Where Jo's power lies with light, yours is in darkness." She handed him a dark circular object that fit in the palm of his hand. He fingered the enigma on the front and his eyes twinkled with a strange dark twilight.

"What do I do with this?" he asked as if in a daze, not looking up from his new trinket.

"Later you won't need it because like Josephine, you'll evolve past the need for an object to project through. For now, I need you to look within and pull out that power in your core, then focus into this medallion," she stated matter-of-factly and pointed to the round disk for emphasis. "Otherwise, we might all get our faces burned off with the untamed power you possess," she said under her breath. "Easy enough?" She clasped her hands together and smiled at the both of us, almost as though she thought that last bit should have been funny. Noise turned our attention back towards the room as the walls began to swell then shrink as if breathing.

The crazy woman stepped further into the room till she was at its center and then

reached into her bag producing an object that looked like an old black book with a bent spine that had some of the pages falling out of it. She cleared her throat, then started reciting words that I couldn't quite make out as the room became darker. I sensed a charge in the air as each bulb began to blow out one by one, sending glass fragments up into the air. She raised her voice so it could be heard over the mini explosions erupting around us and the room, in turn, started to shriek in what sounded to be two different pitches. Damien and I both covered our ears with our hands as we huddled against the back wall. Strong arms and hands emerged from the peeling wallpaper and grabbed my throat, cutting off my air supply. I could see my fiancé out of my peripheral vision, fighting against the possessed walls, trying to free me. I saw his mouth moving but everything was going black.

I felt like Alice falling into the rabbit hole as I spiraled down into shadow. Air blew by me, and I opened my eyes. I had stopped moving, but now I was lying on the floor of the hotel room alone. I slowly got to my feet and I checked my surroundings. It was the same room, but it looked cleaner, or newer maybe? A key in the lock startled me from my distressed state as the handle began to turn. I dove behind the bed and held my breath. I could hear giggling and then the jangling of keys as a man and a woman came into the hotel room. I laid as flat as I could and peered around the side of the bed to get a better look at the couple.

The female had long, bleached blond hair and a short dress that sparkled when she moved. Her high heels clicked across the carpet. The man wore dirty work boots and stained jeans, but he was blurry from the waist up, like he had been pixilated to protect his identity. Both of their voices were muffled; however, I didn't feel I was brought here for the conversation. It was like watching a badly dubbed movie where someone else oversaw the remote. At times they would move in fast forward and then slow down to an odd pace.

Overall, the event was still obvious.

The woman appeared to be an escort based on her demeanor and exchange with the gentleman. I realized somewhere towards the middle of the scene, that the couple couldn't see me and could walk right through me, which was an unpleasant experience I can tell you! I had taken up refuge against the furthest wall to avoid further incident while watching a slow-motion event unfold before me. The female was tied to the bed posts, her feet and legs held by torn sheets of fabric, her dress still on but her shoes off. Her expression seemed less frightened than mine would have been, considering the situation and she had a look of control. Almost as if this plan had been long thought out or maybe her attacker had put her in some kind of trance. The man reached down into his boot and pulled out an object. The woman still smiled as he brought it into view. She probably thought it was harmless, but I could see the weapon from my cowering spot, and I started to cover my mouth for the scream I knew would come.

When the florescent lights hit the shiny object, the victim's eyes widened, and her smile faded. The drama sped up and I covered my face even though I could imagine each sick blow. When I thought it was finally over, I peeked through two fingers to get a glance at the bed. Red would never be a color I would wear ever again after this night's image. The killer was standing over her bound corpse with the bloody dagger. He had a surprised look on his face as if it was the first time he had seen a dead body. He dropped the knife like it was hot to the touch and covered his mouth as though he was about to puke. He looked around the room, like he was seeing it for the first time, and glanced down at his hands drenched in red. This sent him running from the room with a silent scream on his face. I could only imagine what the sound would have been like since this vision had come complete without a volume control, but I was thankful for the silence.

There I was, standing in the corner, alone with the body. I had seen dead people my whole life, but I didn't remember seeing a corpse before. I thought about running after the man, screaming and raving, but where would I go? Into another death dream perhaps? No, there was a reason I had been brought here to see this moment and I would see it through till the end no matter how much it killed me to do it. I moved slowly away from the body towards the exit, tip-toeing the whole way, as if she were only sleeping instead of dead. I hoped to get another glimpse of her killer, or at least catch the vehicle he had been driving the night of the murder to help bring the man to justice.

As I reached the door, I heard gurgling noises from behind me. I carefully turned my eyes to the bed and saw the woman moving. She was still alive! I almost collapsed to the floor. She had a huge gash open across her abdomen that went from one side to the other. I hadn't looked at her before in detail, just enough to think she was dead. With blood pouring down from her mouth like an awful horror movie, she tried to reach her arm out to me but found that her arms were still bound to the posts. How could she see me when they couldn't before? I felt a whoosh go through my body as another man ran through me and blocked my view. Would this nightmare ever end?

I moved to get a better view of this man who I could see details of. He looked panicked as he rushed to her bedside. He had short brown hair and wore a red and blue plaid shirt. The woman was looking up at him as her arm fell away and her eyes grew glassy. The man cried beside her lifeless remains. I drew closer, avoided looking at the woman and instead watched the man. He mourned for her with real emotion in his dark green eyes and I knew then that he must have been her lover. His tears stopped and his gaze became focused on the instrument of destruction lying next to her body. It was still covered in her blood, but he picked it up and held it like he never noticed.

"No, don't do that!" I protested aloud as I watched the man stab himself in the chest.

His eyes were wide and crazy as his body slid to the floor with macabre grace. He laid still, a pool growing around him, the knife still stuck in his chest. I instinctively ran to his side and stood over his torso, looking down at the puddle seeping towards my flip flops. The last sign of life I got from him was the look he gave me before his eyes closed for the last time, a look of love and loss.

Chapter Ten
KNOWLEDGE IS POWER

PEOPLE were shaking me; that much I could tell. I squinted through half shut eyes and noticed that I was outside. Visions of the dead couple still plagued my mind. Who would murder love like that? What man could do such a thing? I wish I could have gotten a good look at him. I felt like Nancy Drew, but I needed to first find clues to solve this mystery. I could hear voices, but they were far away, and their faces were out of focus. A slap hit my face and I began to focus. The mystery lady was standing over me with a smile while Damien stood beside her. I rubbed my cheek gingerly and tried to get up. Damien was there with his arm around me, pulling me to my feet. Sarah ran up and threw her arm around my other side. You would have thought I had sprained an ankle the way I was being treated.

"I must have fainted, guys, no need to overreact." I was still rubbing the offended cheek.

"Jo, you've been out for an hour! We started to take you to the hospital, but the lady insisted this was normal. Another minute and I would have made Steve take us anyway." She looked over to the old lady with a hateful glare. "I told you not to go back in there. You never listen," Sarah rambled clutching my head to her chest.

"You had us terribly troubled child. Tell us what you remember." The older woman suggested.

"We were in the room...creepy stuff started to happen...and then I was in another place. Like I had traveled to another point in time, but I was still in the motel room. The other people there couldn't see me or anything but, I had to watch…I saw…" I trailed off as tears welded up in my eyes. The vision was still too fresh in my mind. I wasn't ready to share just yet.

"What did you see Jo? I knew I should have gone in there with you guys instead of hanging around out here like some coward!" Steve yelled, shaking his fist at no one in particular. Like he could have done anything, anyhow. He would have been another person I would have been responsible for. Why didn't I listen to the warnings? If something had happened to one of my friends, I wouldn't be able to deal with it. Why didn't I tell them what had been happening to me over the past few days so they could have had the option to stick it out with me or have a real vacation? Overwhelming guilt overshadowed the sadness I felt for the dead couple. I can't keep going on like this, worrying everyone and all this crazy stuff with the old lady. I had to put an end to it and take some time to think.

"Look guys, I feel totally drained, and I know you haven't rested at all tonight. Maybe lack of sleep made me see things, but what we need to do is calm down and get a non-haunted room where we might be able to get some sleep. Maybe after a few hours, we can decide what we want to do." If there was a chance for me to slip away while they're sleeping, I'd do it. No long good-byes and no notes. It felt right for me to stay behind and figure this out, but I knew if I said anything to them, they would insist on staying with me.

"You can't be serious Jo! We cannot afford to just ignore this." Damien stated, his arm moving from my waist to my shoulder. He was calling my bluff, so I had to stay in character and act uninterested. I shrugged him off and headed away from the crowd that had formed around me while I was unconscious.

If I could sleep even a little, possibly in the lobby, maybe I would be rested enough to go on the lamb.

"Jo, wait," Sarah pleaded as she ran to catch up. "If you're scared, you can tell me. You know I'm scared, but I 'm your friend that's here to listen. Please, talk to me Jo." She had been my best friend for as long as I could remember. I had to be honest with her no matter what the cost because I owed it to her. I was too overwhelmed to come up with any more excuses anyway.

"All I wanted was for everyone to have a good time. A vacation that we would never forget. Instead, I have endangered my friends, my fiancé, and people I don't even know." I gestured at the two strangers who felt the need to ease drop. "I was warned that this was going to happen and I didn't listen." I hung my head in shame.

"Hold on, you knew this scary stuff was going to happen and you didn't tell me? Your best friend! You can tell me anything, you know that!" Sarah began pacing. "No, I know you, and you would have said something if you knew for sure we would be in danger. After everything we have been through together with your 'special gift'..." She stopped mid-sentence to face me as she pouted like she would explode with tears any minute.

"I didn't know that *this* very thing was going to happen. I thought I was being paranoid about leaving the state for the first time, so I was seeing messages of 'Don't go, stay home,' everywhere. I didn't want to worry you when you do enough for me as it is. You can't get mad at me over this, okay?" I was rambling, barely able to contain the tears from overflowing. I could still leave them to their vacation while I stayed behind and did whatever I had to. I would understand if they wanted nothing more to do with me.

"Mad at you? The only thing I'm mad about is the fact that you didn't tell me. We could have dealt with it together. I love you Jo but you have to put this 'lone wolf' routine to rest. You're stuck with us." The tears rolled down my cheeks as my body felt relief hearing her forgiveness. I suddenly felt like I could faint again. I needed to lay down. Sarah caught me mid stumble. "We need to elevate her legs. I remember seeing a couch in the lobby. Here, help me get her in." Sarah was in control now. I was out and the noises around me were floating away.

I awoke from a dreamless sleep and stretched when my hand brushed against a shoulder. I sat up quickly, adrenaline from the night before still pumping through me.

I sat up to find Damien, slumped over in a sitting position at the end of the couch. He was sleeping soundly so I got up slowly as not to wake him from slumber. Glancing around the room, I saw all my friends lying in odd positions on the scarce furnishings. I tiptoed past them till I reached the door to the outside and gently opened it. I let out the breath I was holding. In the fresh air, my mind cleared of the cobwebs that had formed around my thoughts. How was I ever going to make this up to everyone? They had all been so understanding before and now I had some kind of new ability I had to work out. Before, with my old ability, I didn't have to think to make it work it was just always there. I couldn't remember a time without it. Now I'm going to have to carry weapons and not just talk to the dead but see their deaths. Then there's the strange elderly woman who knows so much and tells us so little. Feeling puzzled and vulnerable, I was unaware that the lady in robes was approaching from behind me.

"Why do you look so worried, child?" she asked innocently as she gestured to sit on the nearby bench.

"I was just thinking about everything that happened last night. I still can't figure out where you came from. How did you know about me? About Damien?" I sat down but was still ready for my "Fight or Flight" mode to kick in if necessary. I was just glad to be angry with someone besides myself. The woman continued to stand to give me space.

"I'm like you, Jo. Sometimes I receive messages. Sometimes I know things. I've trained and worked hard to be open to whatever the universe wants to tell me. But you Jo, are special. Even without training, your power is like nothing I've ever seen. The fact that you and Damien found each other...that's just a magical coincidence."

"I didn't even know Damien was 'special' until you showed up. I still don't understand how you knew." I said accusingly. I was hurt that he hadn't shared with me that he had a curse too. How long had he known?

She shrugged, "I use my spirit guide. She tells me everything I need to know. Your spirit guide should have told you, if your fiancé didn't." She smiled tenderly and slightly turned to her right like she was acknowledging something or someone.

"Wait a second, what is a spirit guide?" I asked now sitting a little closer to the end of the bench to give the crazy woman a seat. She took the hint and her body popped and crackled as she lowered herself onto the seat.

"You've never had a guiding spirit approach you before? By the time I was your age, which seems like a hundred years ago, I had already been contacted by one."

"No, well," I thought of my parents and the honeysuckle smell they left, "do they leave a feeling or a smell behind that makes them different than other spirits?"

"Sometimes. It helps them to make their presence known instead of suddenly appearing. Makes things simpler when you're around 'normies'. You know, people without

talents like ours." She patted me on the knee like I had just been initiated into a special elite club. I thought about this new info and decided that my parents must have been my guides all along. I thought about how happy I was when I saw them in my mind. But they had only ever shown themselves to me in a dream state. Then I remembered their warning that something was coming and how they had helped me against the dark scary man in the kitchen.

"You're thinking hard again. Please, you can speak to me. I only want to help," she said, lightly placing her hand on my shoulder. I contemplated telling her the whole truth but decided against it. No need to give away all my cards and who knew if I could really trust this stranger.

"My parents died in an accident when I was a toddler. I was in the car too but somehow I survived. Since that day, I have always suspected they were watching over me, but now I know they're my guiding spirits."

"Did they ever appear to you?" she asked.

"No, just a feeling I guess." I shrugged.

"The ones that we can't see are a different type of spirit guide. They're experienced through clairvoyance or channeling. They are the ones that people can't find unless they have the 'gift' like we do. Some people use their guides to tell them the future by asking a series of questions. All these questions don't matter to the dead, or even to the big scheme of things. They only answer truthfully to the questions asked about our own paths in life. Otherwise, they play with us when we ask about materialistic things. Will I be rich, that sort of stuff. Should I go down this path or veer in this other direction... these are the questions you should ask your spirit guide." She stopped long enough to check and make sure I was still paying attention. I'm sure my face said how I was feeling. Information overload. "I know you have many questions yourself, why don't you ask me the ones that are plaguing you the most?" She paused to allow me time to gather my thoughts. One big question lingered in the front of my mind.

"Why would your guide look for Damien or me? We don't even know each other. Why spy on us?" I figured that was a fair question she was going to have to answer at some time or another.

"You could say that the dead make good informants since all they do is watch the living. My spirit guide said that you needed my help, so I left my coven and headed out to this dreadful place. Spirit guides can tell you all kinds of useful intel. I'm so relieved that I arrived in time."

"Why would I need your help now? I've been living with this my whole life and when a room tries to eat me and my friends, the 'spirits' finally decide to turn their phantom hands and send a little help?" I was on my feet now, waving my hands agitatedly, as I paced in front of the bench.

"Child, you're all wrapped up in your emotions. Why don't you sit here and try some deep breathing," she said as she patted the seat next to her and started breathing in an odd way. Deep breathing! Here I had a million things all bubbling up inside me and she wanted to show me how to breathe! I could feel the heat of anger in my face, but the strange rhythm of her breath calmed me against my will. Something about her felt so familiar to me. I slowly lowered myself back on to the bench. Why did she have such a soothing effect on me?

"Now just close your eyes and breathe in slowly pulling in cleansing thoughts and push the bad thoughts out when you exhale." I tried it a few times and I realized I could think clearer now then I could before.

"What do we do next?" I asked honestly and with only a hint of anger. Brownie point for me.

"A war is coming. I'm here to help you prepare for it," she stated matter-of-factly and still with a smile on her face.

"War? Between who…?" But I knew the answer before the question could leave my lips. My parents had warned me that 'he' would be coming. Who was this guy and what does he want with me? I looked at the bag lady with newly found recognition on my face.

"You have been well informed, I see. The Trickster comes for you because you are the only one who can get in his way. The rest of us have only been speed bumps to him on his journey to you. Now the time has come for you to face him head on. He is near. I was only able to slow him down." She bowed her head solemnly and I was reminded of the limp she had. I wondered what had happened, but I felt that was a better question for later.

"What's a Trickster? I'm not ready for any war! I just learned more about what I can do. I can't even control it yet! I don't even know what it is!" I was in panic mode again, the breathing exercises completely gone from my memory, scattered in a whirl wind with a thousand other things. I plucked one thought out of the swarm. "Oh my god, we have to get away from here! We don't want to be here for whatever is going to happen! I have to wake up my friends!" I jumped up to run to the lobby doors but the lady in robes grabbed my hand with surprising strength. Her smile had faded, and her eyes had become deep, fathomless black pools.

"He will track you down and find you again. There is nowhere you can go, nowhere you can hide from him forever. He is everywhere and nowhere. Your best bet is to stick with me. I'm the only one who can help you and protect your friends." She knew that last part would persuade me to stay but I still thought about it for a moment before ripping my hand from her grasp. How did I even know what side she was on? What would stop her from throwing me in front like a human shield? How could I trust a stranger with my life and the lives of the only family I had ever known? No way! They had to get out of here even if I stayed.

"How do I know I can trust you? You could be working for 'him' and I will not put my friends in harm's way." I stepped back away from her in case I would have to defend myself. I placed my fists at my sides but in the back of my mind, I knew I would lose against her. The door in front of me flew open and out walked Damien, my fearless rescuer.

"What's wrong?" He seemed to assess the situation. "What's going on, Jo?" He looked between the two of us and I knew he could feel the uncomfortable energy brewing. I glanced down and noticed the hairs on my arms were standing on end. Maybe I did have some power buried deep inside me that I hadn't tapped into yet? I could smell the honeysuckle rising to protect me or serve as a warning. I needed to get a handle on things. I didn't want to cut someone in half just because I was having PMS. This nut ball might hold the key that would release me from this evil entity destiny crap.

"Damien, something is coming, something bad. You're more than welcome to stay and help but we have to get Sarah and Steve away from here while we still can." I wanted so badly to run to him and have him whisk me off to somewhere safe. The sand between our toes and me encircled in his warm arms, just like we had fantasied about in the park. That had only been a few days ago.

"I'm lost! Last night you wanted to run away from this and now you want to stay? You don't even know what you're up against." He gripped both my shoulders like he would shake me to make me better understand, but I knew this gesture as a way to soften his words. I leaned into him, drawing comfort in his arms. My thoughts became more settled as I concentrated on the sound of his heart beating strongly in his chest. I wanted to stay there in that moment but I knew it couldn't last. We had a lot of things going on around us and we would make time for our relationship later, if there was a later. Arrangements needed to be made and there would be more questions. I pulled away from his broad chest and looked up into his eyes.

"I want to explain everything to you, and I know you have a lot to tell me but first, we have to wake the others and get them somewhere safe." He gave me a nod as we both turned towards the door to the lobby. I noticed the bag lady was gone (I still hadn't asked for her name) and I was grateful she had given us a moment to ourselves after the tension had been so high earlier. I had an apology to make to her and I knew it, but we would look for her later. Damien opened the door for me, and I walked into the crisp, cool, air conditioning. Once my eyes adjusted, I realized we were alone in the lobby with nothing more than empty furniture in front of us. Where had everyone gone? "Sarah, Steve! Where are you guys?" I yelled into the empty space.

Chapter Eleven
NOW FOR ANOTHER BRIEF MOMENT OF PANIC BROUGHT TO YOU BY THE LETTER T

"MAYBE they slipped out the side door to the car. I feel like I could use a change of clothes too and our bags are in the car." Damien pinched his shirt at the chest and pulled it towards his nose for a test of its smell. His expression only confirmed it which made me giggle in spite of myself as we headed for the vehicle in hopes of finding our friends. Yes, we were being very calm. There was a reasonable explanation to where our friends had gone. It was better than thinking of the unreasonable ones. After the short trip through the parking lot, we had arrived at our ride only to discover it was still locked and Damien dug the keys from his pocket. We just stared at them in disbelief as we tried to think of another place they would go.

"I guess they didn't go to the car. Where the hell are they?" Damien was looking a little worried about his brother but then a smile came across his face. "I bet they went to find some 'alone' time." He used air quotes to emphasize the 'alone' part like I wouldn't have known what he meant without them. I wasn't convinced that they would sneak out and do something like that after the night we just had but he knew Steve better than I did. He had been acting extra sweet since we started this trip and he and Sarah had been getting seriously closer lately. No, it couldn't be that! Could Steve be planning on proposing? There was no way I was going to have a double wedding! I shook the intrusive thought from my head, there was no other explanation; they had to be in danger!

"We have to find them. I don't know how much longer we have, and something might have happened to them. This is not the time for being 'alone' and having fun!" I yelled using his air quotes roughly before turning on my heel to head back to the motel lobby.

"This is a vacation, Jo. When would be a better time to try and have some fun?" Steve said from out of nowhere causing me to jump and gasp.

"Steve, what the hell man...wait, where's Sarah?" Damien asked quickly glancing around.

"I thought maybe she was with you. I woke-up and everybody was gone. Thought she was in the girl's room but I didn't find her there, then I heard you guys yelling so I came out here." Steve put his hand through the side of his hair and his face fell into concern.

"We were looking for you two. How long do you think she's been missing?" I asked.

"Not long. She couldn't have gone far." Steve and Damien's expressions both looked worried but now I was just plain scared. Where would she have gone without us?

"Standing around here isn't helping! Let's split up. There's a lot of ground to cover but one of us should find her," Damien said. Steve turned and retraced his steps back the way he had come. Damien walked off towards the dumpster and tree lined area that separated the motel from the restaurant next door. That only left the long stretch of one floor rooms for me to check.

First, I thought about going door to door asking if anyone had seen my friend Sarah who might have gotten lost. It took only a minute to realize what a stupid idea that was. I couldn't picture myself as a threat to anyone that was willing to stay the night in such a rundown shack of a motel voluntarily, but I knew they could be a threat to me. By the way the parking lot appeared, I expected to see leather clad men with bad hat hair and a sorry disposition for helping lost women. I chose instead, to go down the line of doors, listening for the 'sounds of Sarah' and hoping not to disturb anyone. I could smell the salt water on the breeze, and I thought of how we had come all this way and hadn't put one toe in the crystal-clear blue water of the ocean yet. Maybe Sarah and Steve could go and enjoy the sights (if we found her) while Damien and I stayed behind to fight the 'big bad', whatever it was.

I reached the walkway that passed the rows of doors to my right. The overhang above me was tilted and light from above shown through tiny slits that formed an odd picture on the concrete below. As I walked, bright shapes danced along my tank top and shorts, like broken shards of glass bouncing off into different directions. I needed to be on the alert, prepared for anything in case it strikes. A sound behind me made me tense up but I didn't turn around. Instead, I balled my hands into fists and instinctively the energy around me shifted. At least that part of my powers seemed easy and all I had to do was breath in deeply for the power to build within myself. I turned, prepared, but only discarded paper fluttered behind me. I would have turned it into ash had I not stopped myself. I envisioned what I had done to the bathroom door and I felt that surge of energy in my hands. Little noises were going to be a distraction and I needed to focus on only Sarah and not my own paranoia.

Tuning my ears to pick up sounds of distress, I continued my journey down the concrete alley. Some rustling came from within a few rooms, but none of them sounded like Sarah. Why would she be in any of the rooms anyway? Unless someone was hiding her to torture me. I pushed that thought away, I had enough dark imagines in my mind already. Why didn't she just stay in the lobby? I peered to my left to see if any of my friends had made any progress only to see Steve coming out of the lobby empty-handed again and Damien making his way over to me. Where else was there to look? What monster could have lured her from Steve's protective embrace into a catacomb of chaos we were spiraling into? She is the sweet and helpless center of our group. Steve appeared beaten and discouraged. I wanted to smile reassuringly at his sad face, but I knew I would fail to make it genuine. I loved Sarah too and I didn't want to imagine not having her around. What will I do if I don't find her?

An unexplainable sensation went through me causing my body to shiver and my feet to stop. It felt like fingers probing me on my right side which happened to be parallel to the motel doors. The sensation felt vaguely familiar to me as I felt the presence. I glanced down at my arms where the hairs were standing straight up. Out of the corner of my eye, I saw Damien approach but stop and examining his arms as well. Apparently, we both had felt the phantom fingers.

Steve had just made it over to us. "What are you guys doing? Do you hear Sarah?" he asked in a panic.

"No, but I think I just felt her. Jo, did you feel that?" Damien turned to me questionably.

"I don't know. It was like I could sense her, almost smell her or something. I think it came from that way," I pointed down the corridor and we all sprinted that way.

"But which room...?" Steve's question was interrupted as we came to a holt in front of the door we had left cracked last night. He didn't hesitate but instead walked right by us into the room, wildly looking around for Sarah.

"Sarah, you had us all scared! What are you doing?" We could hear him ask. I poked my head around the corner and briefly glanced around the room, hesitant to return inside again. The murder I had seen there was still fresh in my mind and I didn't want to relive it so soon. Upon brief inspection, I noticed Sarah sitting on the floor moving her hand just in front of the wall instead of touching it, not that I blamed her. Steve was beside her staring into her emotionless face. Damien gently stepped past me into the room, and I felt him go still while he stared at the two on the floor.

"Why isn't she answering me? What is she doing?" Steve asked deeply concerned waving a hand in front of Sarah's face.

"She's sensing a presence of course," said the old lady as she walked out of the bathroom, drying her hands on a towel.

"What the hell have you done to Sarah?" Steve yelled as he came to his feet and started towards the lady. Damien regained his composure and stopped his brother from tackling the frail older woman.

"I haven't done anything! Jo wanted to protect her friends because they couldn't protect themselves. Now, Sarah is no longer helpless, and she can aide you in your journey using her new ability," she said in her defense.

"Like Damien?" I asked eyeing her suspiciously. Why is it that this lady had popped into our lives and suddenly everyone could do some amazing trick? I didn't want to be responsible for making my friends freaks and I wanted to make her accountable for these new abilities. "You *giving* them these 'talents' doesn't change anything! Now they'll just be bigger targets for whatever's coming!" Everyone but Sarah turned to me at that. Right now, I only had eyes for the old woman.

"You think I am giving them their powers? Why child, I am only dusting off the surface and shinning a small bit of light on their potential. Only they can choose to accept the possibility that nothing happens on accident. We were all put into this room, at this very moment, for a purpose. Destiny, if you want to call it that. I'm here to help you all get control of your inner selves. That's my purpose here. Damien is your protector and Sarah is here to help you track down what you need."

"My purpose will be to kick your ass for what you've done to Sarah!" Steve was up in her face; all the sweet words she had said were falling on deaf ears. I stole a glance at Sarah and noticed the distance in her gaze as her hand traced a pattern up the wall without touching it. It appeared like she was sketching in mid-air.

"Sarah has consented to this procedure, all I did was point her in the right direction. Here, you can ask her yourselves." We all turned our attention back to Sarah on the floor where she was beaming up at us. Steve knelt back down beside her.

"It's true! She told me that I had this gift in me too that would help everyone. Honestly, I didn't believe her at first, but wow!" she said breathlessly. "I didn't know it could be like this!" She was acting as giddy as a kid on Christmas morning, eager to take her new bike out for a spin. If it was possible for her to have leapt out of her skin, she would have.

"But, are you okay? You seemed like you were somewhere else there. You feel alright?" Steve was treating her like a mental patient just released but she just patted him on the shoulder and smiled.

"Don't worry Steve, I'm fine. I just kind of go away for a minute when I do it, it's hard to explain, but it doesn't hurt and it's no trouble to get back. I'm still the same huggy bear you always knew," she playfully poked him in the ribs. He smiled back at her, all his worries erased from his face.

"What is it you can do?" Damien asked. I was glad he had because I wasn't sure if my voice would have held out for the question. Deep down I was hiding anger and surprise from my face. This strange, odd woman was ruining everything! Only I had to be sacrificed before, but now she had dragged my friends in with me by promising to unlock their 'potentials'. I never needed help, I liked it better when they were defenseless. They wouldn't be reluctant to get out of the way when things got bad but now there would be more kindling for the fire. Sarah got up from the floor with Steve's help.

"I can sense the presence of power. I can tell how old it is, how strong it is, and as you all were approaching, I could tell how close you were. I'm like a magical tracker! Marge showed me how to release this energy I had locked up in me and project it in front of me like a finger. Then it became a hand as I focused it. I can tell you everything about this room if you want! There are two entities here, they're over 20 years old, and they are both very strong with anger!"

"I guess I would be too if I was dead," Steve interrupted.

"How can you tell that they are angry?" Damien asked ignoring him.

"It makes my arm tingle to touch the auras around the walls. It's almost like red ants crawling up them. Their essence has left a mark here in this room, too, telling me that one is female and the other is male. Isn't this exciting? I can help you now!" Sarah's smile widened and it truly favored the Cheshire

Cat. I even felt a little like Alice again, wandering into a world that I didn't understand but with time, could navigate smoothly. If only there was an "Eat Me" cookie lying around somewhere so I could shrink and run away before this "Trickster" finds me and my band of misfits.

Nothing was going the way I planned so far. Not that I could have planned for this! I'd been with Sarah so long and never once did she exhibit any signs of a special ability nor had Damien. How come I never once noticed how special they all were? Maybe that was how they had all accepted me so easily. Damien's attention had turned to me unnoticed while I was deep in thought. I could only hope my face didn't reflect what I was feeling. I didn't want to explain myself to him until I had become more collected. He touched my shoulder lightly, but he didn't say anything, only waited for me to respond to Sarah's excitement. Steve was beside Sarah examining her hands like he expected to see what she was talking about on them.

"That's really a useful quality you have there, Sarah," I said dumbly with only a hint of sarcasm. Another brownie point for me. Steve cleared his throat.

"So do I have something in me too?" he asked, first looking at Sarah and then at the bag lady whose name was just discovered to be Marge.

"I don't know, do you?" she asked back with a smile.

"I think I do," he stated, "but what is it? Is it like what Damien has? No, I bet it's better," Steve smirked.

"You will find it out on your own, Steven, but I can tell you that it will be marvellous." She looked to her left like she was acknowledging someone else again. I wondered if that was where her spirit guide resided. Why couldn't I see her spirit guide? If I could see spirits in general, then why not hers? That only made me more suspicious of her. Definitely a question I would have to ask her later.

"We don't have time for this, Steve. Jo said there was something coming for her, so we need to get the hell out of Dodge, like now!" I could see the eagerness in Damien's eyes to be done with all of this and on the road away from the approaching danger. He was worried about me, but what he didn't know was that I was more worried about him. After this evil killed me, what would stop it from hurting my family?

"Maybe I can help using my new ability!" Sarah stated.

"Can you do that?" I asked, surprised at how stable my voice sounded.

"Sure. I felt you and Damien when you approached, and I could tell it was you two. It's just like stretching out an arm." She looked over at the older woman and they exchanged a look that was just between the two of them. Sarah closed her eyes and creased her forehead with concentration. She moved her arms out from her body. "Could you guys get behind me with Steve? I need to focus and all I can feel is you two." She smiled a bit with her eyes still closed while Damien and I took our places behind Steve. What an odd scene for someone to come up on as they're leaving their rooms. Here was an old lady leaning against a wall watching three people huddled behind a girl that appeared to be blind and trying to find her way around. Would it look like we were hiding in the one place she wasn't looking in a Marco Polo game gone wrong? I could only imagine.

We were all holding our breaths, afraid we would distract her by making any noise. The 'Marge' lady seemed to be the only one in the room that was not worried about what was going on before her. I knew I would never get used to any of this. Did nothing surprise her anymore? How much had her ancient eyes seen? I wondered if Damien would be able to cope when I could not. What about Sarah or Steve who already seemed okay and comfortable with the things that were going on? We were advancing too quickly for my tastes and my thoughts kept returning to Marge's role in everything. She was looking guiltier to me every minute.

Sarah's eyes flew open in triumph. "I think I've found him... or them. It feels old and new. Why is that? Something else is with them but...I can't see it. Like it's blocking me." The lines between her brows creased further as she looked up at the older lady expecting an answer.

"How close are they, dear, could you tell?" she asked in her strangely sweet voice.

"They're just a few miles out, I think. It's still kind of hard to judge distance, so I suppose that would be a guess." She allowed her hands to fall back to her sides. Steve put his arms around her from behind and pressed a kiss to her hair which appeared damp with sweat. We all stood there in silence, expecting whoever or whatever it was coming after us to walk through the door at any minute wielding a medieval axe. But who is it that 'he' brought with him? Would we be able to stand against an army of experienced bad guys bent on our destruction? Why stop at just us? Why not the world? A feeling of dread raged within me. Damien stood closer to me and lightly ran his fingers along my bare arm comfortingly. With him by my side, how could I not be brave? We had overcome families and our hellish childhoods. This would be a piece of cake, but I couldn't even convince myself.

"We should move. You're welcome to ride along," I told Marge grudgingly. I had a renewed sense of purpose, but we needed her, no matter my misgivings.

"Why thank you, that would be lovely," she answered in a tone that was inappropriately light.

"So we're just going to run?" Steve asked, suddenly the brave one.

"No...but we can't fight here, bro. Too many bystanders," Damien replied. What were we doing, going to war? Without another word, we made our way back to the lobby to retrieve or few belongings from the night before.

"Are you leaving so soon?" asked the manager after Damien had received our reimbursement from the room from hell. None of us answered him but I turned to give him a look as I left. What a ridiculous question to ask someone after the night we'd had. We worked in silence, reloading our belongings into the trunk before taking our seats in the vehicle. Steve and Sarah were bunched up in the back with Marge in her voluminous robes next to them looking out the window occasionally. I glanced back to make sure everyone was settled in when I noticed Sarah smiling back at me. I turned back to Damien in the captain's chair where he was still in deep concentration, gazing out the windshield as he started the car.

The motel was slowly disappearing from view which made me relax and unclench my fists. I knew we would be safe once we had some distance between us and the haunted room but how long would it be before trouble found us again? Would our enemy find us anywhere we went, could he or they track us? A handful of people knew where we were going to go when we left for Spring Break and we didn't leave the desk manager with our names or destination, so how could he be tracking us? Perhaps Marge had been right, and we would never truly be safe again until he's defeated.

"Will we ever rest again?" I whispered to no one in particular. Damien reached out and took my hand, squeezing it tightly. That was the closest contact his seat belt would allow, but it was enough. He continued to look back through the rearview mirror. Steve noticed his brother's demeanor and turned around to look out the back.

"I think we're being followed, bro!" Steve yelled pointing his finger for emphasis. I heard a belt snap into place from the back as I tugged on my own to make sure it was secure. With a glance in my side mirror, I saw nothing unusual. There was a tractor trailer coming up on us fast but that wasn't strange. I expected a car or a motorcycle; something easy to maneuver to be darting somewhere from behind it. I faced the back window for a better view. Sure enough, the only thing following us was a huge semi-truck driving wildly up the middle of the yellow line.

"You think it's them?" Steve asked Sarah as I looked on confused.

"It's them," she said also facing the back window. An eerie presence now hovered over us, surrounding the vehicle.

"In the semi?" I asked still not understanding.

"Maybe we could lose him at the turnabout ahead!" yelled Steve, ignoring me entirely.

"A truck that size won't be able to maneuver a turn like that. It just might work," Damien said as he jerked the wheel to the left. We took the curve so fast, we were like a ball on a roulette wheel. Thank God for seatbelts. The tractor trailer followed in hot pursuit though the turn, and it did make it fall behind, so we tried to find a good turn off to take. To the right was a one-way street that would dump us onto a busy road. At least that route would get us among other people where it would be hard for the semi to follow.

"Take this right, Damien!" I yelled uncertain if we would miss our opportunity to reach safety. Damien twisted the wheel to the right and miraculously the car didn't flip. We rubbed the right rim on the curb as we made the turn, but the rest of the car was unscathed. I turned to see if the driver of the truck would be so lucky as to make the turn but was distracted as the old lady pulled a jar from her bag. She whispered to it before tossing it out the window into the path of the speeding truck.

"What the hell was that?" Damien yelled the question over his shoulder.

"It's nothing, just a glass mason jar, deary," she stated, full of mystery.

"*Why* did you throw it out the window, I think is the real question Damien was asking," Sarah replied.

"It should slow them down before they hurt someone. I didn't want that awful man to get close to your nice car. How would we ever get anywhere then?" She brushed the question off like it wasn't an odd thing to see an elderly woman tossing things out of moving vehicles. What was a broken jar going to do to a semi anyway? If it had at least splattered onto the windshield, it could have temporally distracted him.

"Hang on guys!" Damien yelled over his shoulder as we merged into the busy traffic. I whipped back around to watch his progress as cars honked around us.

"Wow, look at that!" Steve said excitedly. He turned towards the bag lady, failing to mention what he saw. "You have to show me how you did that!"

"All in good time, dear. There's more where that came from." I whipped around to see what the fuss was about. The truck wasn't behind us anymore and the old lady was smirking. What the heck did she do?

Chapter Twelve
STUCK!
Frank

"YOU let them get away, you imbecile!" The voice bounced around angrily in Frank's head.

"I didn't mean to," Frank responded. He hung his head in shame thinking that he had made it all this way and still the voice was displeased with him. He hoped this would be his last journey with the intruder in his skull. Its yelling only reminded him of the countless years he had held its secret. Why did he deserve such endless torture? It was because of the voice he did bad things.

"*I'm* being tormented here, Frankie boy! Rattling around inside your vacant skull!" It wasn't the first time he'd been insulted by the voice invading his thoughts. He couldn't remember ever hearing a nice word from the voice, regardless of his obedience. "Would you like me to pat your head and feed you a treat too?" mocked the cruel intruder continuing to read Frank's thoughts.

The trucker just wanted the books to reflect his victories that far outweighed his failures. It was probably too much to ask a disembodied voice. Frank unbuckled his seat belt and wedged the driver's side door open. There was a limited amount of space down the one-way and he remembered plainly telling the voice that they wouldn't fit down its narrow passage, but the voice insisted and down the alley they went, only to get stuck.

"We wouldn't be stuck here, you idiot, if not for that meddling old woman and her jars!" Frank thought the voice had really lost it this time, as he squeezed out of the opening in the door next to the brick wall. He proceeded to the front of his rig. Light wisps of smoke came from the grill, and he could feel the heat rolling off the engine. He thought to himself, how lucky they were to keep up with that car and make the turnabout without killing themselves or someone else.

He resisted the urge to place his hands on the hood and soothe the semi as you would an overheated spouse. As he neared the passenger side, he noticed a large amount of pinkish gunk on the wheels and the brick walls beside them. He threw up his hands to either side of his head much like a terrified woman would do in a B horror movie. There was more of the goo all over the side fender and clinging down the trailer. "How in the hell..." he said aloud pushing his hat up and scratching his forehead.

"The witch's magic may have slowed us down, but it hasn't stopped us completely," said the angry voice.

"How do we get this stuff off?" asked Frank.

"Leave it to our new friend to clean it up," answered the voice. Frank turned and jumped when he noticed the big black dog standing silently behind him. On the ride over, it never once stuck its head out the window and wagged its tongue in the breeze, convincing Frank that it was definitely a hellhound. It never even stuck its tongue out and breathed heavily beside him. This animal was unnaturally quiet. Had he even heard it approach?

"Now, my servant," said the voice using Frank's mouth and avoiding his questions completely, "our enemies are escaping! You must clear this garbage off so we can be on our way again." After the last word fell from his mouth, the obedient dog walked over to the goo and sniffed it. This was the first 'dog like' thing he had seen it do. Frank stumbled back with a startled look after he heard the monster growl deep within its throat. The sound worked its way up and out the creature's mouth and came forth loudly as a belch accompanied by a thick fog. Rings, as clear as smoke, pulsated from within the cloud and smacked the gummy substance which made a sound like a belly flop gone badly. The impact blew some of the substance off the truck's surface. Some was still holding on the wheels, but Frank thought he could jump in his rig and easily get her going. He turned his back on the scene and headed towards the driver's side door. As he reached for the handle, he heard a sound of metal tearing. Fearing for his ride, he ran towards the sound but only found the mongrel staring up at him while he smacked his jaws like a dog with gum in its mouth. He stole a glance behind the creature and noticed the goo was gone without a trace of it left.

"How'd he do that?" asked the trucker now dumbfounded, but he knew he wouldn't get an answer. He could have sworn the beast laughed at him.

"Let's get back on the road before they're too far ahead of us," the skull visitor said reasonably, all traces of the earlier fury gone. Frank obeyed and was back behind the steering wheel in seconds. He allowed the hound to go in before him since there was no room for the passenger side door to open. The dog hiccupped once in the cab which made the trucker chuckle to himself as he turned the keys in the ignition. The engine didn't turn over and Frank tried again to no avail. His heart sank as he pictured the beast gnawing on his motor to repair it like he had the wheels. He could see in his mind, parts in shreds on the ground and sparks coming from pieces that Frank didn't even know existed or how they worked. It had to turn over!

He pumped the gas pedal as he turned the key, praying his baby wouldn't be turned into a scrapheap before his eyes. He gave the dashboard a little love tap in the hope of bringing the rig to life but he only heard laughter coming from the voice. 'What's so funny,' Frank thought. He felt like having a heart attack right here as panic gripped his chest.

"Please, come on," he begged aloud and sure enough, the engine started right up. Frank let out a rush of air as he checked that his cap concealed his face and his seat belt and mirrors were in place. He felt a wave of relief as he started down the one way slowly, carefully merging with the traffic ahead.

"Which way do you think they went?" he asked out loud even though he didn't need to.

"I'm not sure," the voice answered in his head, "but we'll find them. Just make a right up ahead off the road and we shall inspect the map." Frank obeyed, as he so often did and turned right next to the JCT 121 sign. Shortly after that, they were parked at a Subway gas station combo with their map in hand.

"How's the map going to help when we don't know what direction they went?" asked the driver to his rearview reflection.

"The fewer questions you ask the less stupid you will look," replied the mirror. Frank's arm moved involuntarily towards the beast's neck beside him. He didn't want to touch the monster, but his hand moved anyway. He watched in horror as he undid a clasp buried in the beast's fur and held it up. Dangling from his hand was a collar with a small, clear jewel the likes of which he had never seen. Even though there was no direct sunlight in the cab, the orb shone as brightly as a million stars. Frank's other hand moved the map towards the orb but it tugged back a little towards his chest.

"Don't fight me, not now!" the voice yelled through his reflection.

"Will it hurt?" the truck driver asked now fearful of this shining treasure and the beam that seemed to come from it.

"No, you moron! Now let go!" Frank obeyed and the map went under the crystal which started spinning around in circles.

"I picked up this little trick from The Traveler along with his dog." Who was the Traveler? Frank wanted to ask but he knew he would only be answered in mean words and harsh tones. "Once they make a decision of where they are going, we will be able to tell which way to go." The trucker watched the hypnotic rhythm of the jewel as it moved. The crystal stopped spinning and made quick lines in a downward motion.

"Ah ha, we must start heading southwest! Stupid mortals must be heading for food or rest and that's when we'll have them!" The trucker didn't think that eating sounded like such a bad thing at all for he was sleepy and hungry.

"Oh, if you must...I suppose we have time for you to stop at the next fast food distributor for caffeine and nourishment. I swear this body has been more trouble than the century I spent having small amounts of acid dropped on my head as punishment for some...minor misdeed." The intruder rattled off.

The truck driver smiled at the idea of the voice being tortured as he placed the map back in the glove compartment. The collar, he laid beside the animal because he was too afraid to wrap his hands around the beast's neck once more. He was at least getting a warm meal and coffee in his guts, even though he had to continue a path of murder and chaos. The ultimate goal was still something Frank had yet to discover but if it was going to be anything like it was before, someone would be dead, and Frank would be the one with the blood on his hands.

They stopped at a fast food joint where he was able to purchase two greasy sandwiches and a delicious cup of black coffee from inside. He juggled the items carefully as he made his way back to the cab. He unwrapped a breakfast sandwich and laid it slowly down next to the monster. After all, he was an animal of some kind, and all that bubble gum stuff couldn't have filled him up well.

"What are you doing? The Travelers dog never eats...or drinks or sleeps for that matter! You mortals know nothing!" Frank thought that maybe there was a book somewhere he had forgotten to read that would have been titled, 'So now You Have a Devil Dog' but the job at hand would have to be done first, of course, before he could even think about going to the library. The trucker took a big bite of the already unwrapped sandwich and sipped his coffee thoughtfully. Soon the sandwich was gone, and he was unwrapping the next one as he started up his rig and began the trip southwest.

"This will be the last time and then I will be rid of the both of you, right? That was the deal," he said out loud to his reflection as he checked his mirrors. There had to be a way to get rid of the voice, but he couldn't think of one. He was answered with more laughing as the truck took its final turn back to the main road. Frank thought about how crazy he had become. Talking out loud to a voice only he could hear. How much longer could he take of this before he went completely mad?

Chapter Thirteen
OLD LADIES IN CLOWN CARS?
Jo

SILENCE had fallen over the car of young people and one old woman for quite a few miles. I had been deep in thought over what had happened back in the alley with the truck driver. Was it just a coincidence that a semi killed my parents, and one was chasing after us? Could it be the same man? Why hadn't the police found him? Was he here to finish the job he started twenty-one years ago? Round and round the questions went, without any answers.

Maybe, I thought, if we found a safe place, I could ask Marge what she knew about me and what happened to my bio parents. Maybe she would be able to ask her spirit guide and give me a clue to why all this was happening to me.

"Damien, I've got to go to the girl's room. Can we pull over at that truck stop ahead? I saw a sign a little ways back...it should be right up here," Sarah said reaching over the backseat pointing. We had crossed the state line into Louisiana without a break for hours. I needed to stretch my legs, but I feared that if we stopped, even for a moment, they would find us again. The blue sign for the truck stop appeared on the right and Damien eased over.

"Do you think we should stop?" I asked Damien.

"Steve and I can pee in bottles, but unless you and Sarah want to try that, we don't have much of a choice." He quickly realized how harsh he had sounded so he reached over and held my hand. "We'll be in a public place. I'll be on the lookout the whole time, okay?" It was stupid to be afraid of a rest stop, but I was terrified that they would find us. There was no way the driver could have known which direction we went. Damien was right, it would be fine. I nodded to him in agreement, and he turned into a parking spot. He killed the engine while we sat in silence, reluctant to move. I felt a cramp in my calf starting like I had tensed up my muscles during the last few miles. Maybe we could make this quick enough that it wouldn't give up our lead on our crazy truck driving stalker.

"Dude, there's no need to be such a downer! The lady threw some magical goo back there that I guarantee slowed that guy down! It was some grade A, out of this world stuff!" Steve piped in from the back clamping a big hand down on his brother's shoulder.

"It only slowed them down. But the coven has things to stop them in their tracks. We'll put him back where he belongs," Marge said reassuringly.

"I thought I saw just one guy? Is there going to be more like that?" Steve asked picking up on the pronouns.

"Uh, maybe we should hurry before we lose our lead on them," Sarah said, squirming slightly from a full bladder. We all exited the car together and Sarah and I headed to the ladies room with our new older friend. I had a strange sense of deja vu as we entered yet another rest stop restroom since our journey began just yesterday. We had been so excited then, only to hear that our hotel had caught fire. The whole chain of events seemed overwhelming and lacking coincidence.

Sarah raced over to the nearest stall. I went to the sink to splash cold water on my face to get rid of any leftover make-up from our hellacious night before. The reflection staring back at me didn't look like me at all. My hair stuck up in odd places from beneath my ponytail and I had dark circles under my eyes from lack of sleep. I felt yucky gazing at myself. I looked like a scared rabbit so I stuck my tongue out just for some comic relief. I was stronger than this. I had to be brave, not just for my friends, but for myself. Sarah had caught my reflection as she came out of the stall.

"I hope that tongue wasn't for me," she said as she approached the mirror and pulled out her make-up bag.

"I know there must be some miracle concealer in there." I said holding out my hand.

She looked me over. "I don't think I brought enough make-up for what the two of us need." We both smiled despite how scared we were, at least we still had our sense of humor.

"So when we get back out there and on the road, where will we go? Spring Break only lasts a week, and I don't want to be late for our first day back." She honestly believed we would have this whole matter resolved in just a few days; she must be joking.

"You're not serious, are you Sarah? You don't really believe that we could just go back to school, back to our normal lives. After all that we've witnessed! I know you're not that naive." I regreted the words as soon as they came out of my mouth, but it was too late, and now they just hung in the air of silence and flushing toilets.

After an eternity, Sarah said, "I guess I was talking without thinking. I'm just so tired of being scared and surprised at every turn," she pouted. "I keep thinking I can just go home, and everything will be like it was before." She threw a tube of something back in her bag and wrapped her hands around her elbows.

"Where I'm the only freak, I can live with that. It would be great if we could just go back to the way things were! I don't want to think about the possibility of one of you getting hurt." I plucked out her pink lipstick from the bag just to have something to fidget with.

"You know you're not the only one that can take care of herself! I remember a life before I met you, my *big* protector, and I did just fine!" She took the lipstick from my hand and applied some to her mouth.

"I didn't mean to offend your highness," I said with a curtsey. "Really, you know I just meant that alone, I can take care of myself, which is easier, but you're right, and I need to accept that you are all adults capable of making your own decisions." I waved my hands in the air to show I was backing off.

She looked at me and smiled before saying, "See, talking things out helps. Doesn't it?"

"You are right again, oh wise one," I replied smartly. Sarah kept me from being eaten up with guilt which is more than I could have ever asked in a friend. I knew the boys could take care of themselves, but I always felt like I had to look out for poor little Sarah who never ceased to surprise me. She proved time and again that you can't judge a book by its cover.

"So, do you have any clues who this guy is stalking us?" Sarah asked combing through her hair.

"I don't have enough evidence to even make a guess right now. But I know he's a bad guy that we don't want to mess with until we know for sure what we are dealing with." I took out my rubber band and shook my hair loose.

"Yeah, I guessed that, but what does he want from us? Is he after you because you're 'special'?" She whispered to avoid further stares from the adults coming in and out of the stalls. She was ever vigilant with her new detective-like attitude but she had a right to all her questions.

"He's called a 'Trickster' or something; still working that out, which is a name some ghosts gave me. I didn't want to tell you before, but I saw one our final day at school. I think that trucker or 'Trickster' guy, is the same one that killed my parents." Sure I had messed up the order of events and all the details but it had been a long couple of days. At least I was truthful. Sarah walked over and placed a comforting hand on my shoulder. She would understand why I left out the part about seeing them and the message I received. It felt like the more people I told, the less magic there would be for me to return to that place. Silly, I know, but I wouldn't take a chance on not seeing them again.

"Are you sure he's the one that killed them, Jo? Gosh, I hadn't even thought of that."

"Yeah, but why come after me now?" I asked placing my hand on my hip and sticking it out.

"When you left the state, you lost the protection of my coven I sent for you," the old witch announced as she walked out of a stall. The two of us jumped a mile high when she spoke, we had totally forgot she had come in with us. Wait, was she on the toilet this whole time? Jeez.

"*Your* coven has been protecting me all these years? How do you even know me?" It seemed like every conversation with this lady began with how or why.

"I told you about our spirit guides. They are very helpful finding things, especially powerful things. In this situation, it turned out to be you, which surprised us as well. We hadn't expected you to become this powerful and exhibit such potential at this young age." She placed her bag on the counter and turned on the water to start washing her hands.

"You've known about me this whole time? Why didn't you come to me sooner instead of letting me learn about my abilities alone? Do you know how hard it is to have this gift with no one to share it with? No one to explain and help me control it? I wouldn't have felt like a freak in hiding!" I turned away from the old hag so she wouldn't see the emotion on my face. How could she? How could they? I'd been struggling this whole time with who I am and why I'm different when, not that far away, someone else knew. I was so filled with both anger and sorrow when Sarah came over to stand in front of me, that I wasn't sure which emotion she was responding to.

"You would have never met me or any of the other kids at Momma D's if you had been taken to a coven. Just think of all the things we would have missed had we not met." Sarah was right, as usual, but I still had this feeling of abandonment. Would my life really have been easier if I had lived in a coven instead of in a loving environment surrounded with other kids who knew the pain of losing a parent like I did? In a strange way, I had far more in common with them than with Marge. That thought gave me comfort and strength.

"I know you can see why we didn't come for you right away. Can't you, Josephine?" Marge looked at me as she dried her hands.

"I suppose my experiences helped shape me into who I am today. Still, a guiding hand would have been helpful," I replied. This was all so overwhelming, but I could feel my shoulders relaxing as the anger began to subside.

"What's the plan? What do we do next?" Sarah asked surprisingly breaking the discomfort in the air.

"First things first, my dears. We must put distance between us and them until we have found our way to my coven for training. There, we'll be protected until we're prepared to fight."

"Where is the coven?" I asked.

"We have been a group on the run for many years. We have been everywhere across this great country; prepared to pick up and go when needed. I don't have a destination, only a direction."

"How will we find them, then?" asked Sarah looking concerned.

"I know how to find them," she answered.

"But you just said you don't really know where they are. We can't waste time driving around until we spot them." I stated.

"There are ways of finding things that you don't know the location of. I will show you. Have faith and follow me," she said as she turned and walked out the bathroom door.

"Should we do this?" Sarah whispered. "I mean it sounds like we have a tight schedule." There was my organized, in control girl back again.

"Well, she's the only one that can tell us where to go and learning these skills is apparently the difference between life and death. It isn't like we have a choice," I answered. We both took one last look at our droopy reflections and headed out the door behind Marge and her gigantic bag of tricks.

Once outside, we signaled to the boys at the car that we would just be a moment longer before following our resident witch to a tall tree, near the edge of the rest stop's green space. A few picnic tables and rusted grills were scattered amongst the trees where weary truckers walked cement paths. The older lady placed her bag on the ground next to the tree and put her free hands up in the air with her eyes closed.

"Should we be mimicking her pose?" whispered Sarah.

"Do I look like I know what she's doing?" I whispered back. Marge's arms came slowly down to her sides as she turned to look at the two of us.

"I was cleansing the area around us. You never know who is turning into the same channel you're using. Now, I need both of you on either side of me to balance out the energy." The crazy woman turned so that her back was to the tree while Sarah and I went to stand on either side of her. She bent over suddenly and grabbed a handful of dirt from under the tree and held it up to her face. Sarah and I exchanged glances that read, 'I hope she's not going to eat that.' She threw it out in front of her where we saw the shape of an arrow in the falling earth.

"What in the world was that?!" I asked in astonishment.

"That, my dears," she said pointing her finger in the direction the arrow had been pointing, "is the way to my coven. Let's get in the car and start going in that direction." A few minutes later, Sarah and I had made it back into the car and were briefly describing what we had seen back at the tree.

"But how is that even possible?" Damien repeated for the umpteenth time.

"Man, this lady is pretty wicked! You didn't see what happened back there with the jar. This woman has got some kind of power!" Steve said jumping up and down in his seat like an excited child on his way to Disney. No wonder the old woman hadn't said what Steve's power was since it's obviously the power of annoyance.

"Shh, here she comes," Sarah said, nudging her boyfriend as the older lady approached the car from the bathrooms. She probably had to rinse her mouth out from all the dirt talking she had been doing. A hush fell inside the car as Marge climbed in, her robes filling the backseat.

"As I'm sure you boys know by now, we need to head further west. If I know my gals, they'll have supper waiting for us when we get there." I was happy to hear that we wouldn't be traveling that much further because it was already noon and the car was beginning to smell ripe in the heat. I didn't think my nerves could last for days on end in a cramped car full of BO. It wouldn't be good on my butt either for sure.

Belts clicked and then the engine fired. We were in our small vessel of refuge; surrounded by others escaping their lives in metal containers. This time was different because we had a plan, but it didn't help the butterflies I felt in my stomach. I made quick glances at the rearview mirror, checking to see if there was a shining reflection of a familiar speeding semi.

Deciding to borrow some of Marge's positivity, I held Damien's hand and tried to picture the moment we would reach the coven, the moment I could unclench and relax. It might give me a chance to meditate and catch a word with my parents. Hopefully, they would be up to answering some questions involving Marge, this crazy old lady in heavy robes and her relation to the mad trucker. I knew it could not have been coincidence they both showed up at the same time. There had been nothing but trouble since their arrival and they've left me with nothing but more questions. Then again, Marge wasn't the one who was trying to kill us, and she was trying to be helpful, even if it was in a very mysterious way.

I thought back to the hotel room and the weird phenomenon that took place. I knew Damien and I needed to sit down and have a heart to heart about his part in what had happened. He had taken to his ability so well, almost like it was familiar to him. Which meant he had been hiding a piece of himself from me. I tried to convince myself to give him the benefit of a doubt and not be so quick to order a firing squad. I hadn't told him about the warnings I had been receiving regarding our trip. No sense in casting the first stone. Once we got to the coven, we could learn the answers to all the important questions. Until then, we needed to watch our backs in case trouble showed up again.

We turned down a narrow, two-lane road off the interstate which ran west, and we started seeing signs for towns. How would we know which one of these exits to stop at? Which town was our destination? My stomach growled which startled me in the silent car. It had been hours since we had been at the motel and even longer since we had eaten. Other growls echoed mine like I had started a communication between our stomachs, but it only meant that we were all hungry and needed to stop somewhere. This time last week, I had pictured us having our first lunch much differently. Now, we would have to put up with a dull meal of fried foods and tired company.

"Anyone in the mood for something in particular?" Sarah asked looking around for a restaurant sign off the lonely highway.

"Fast and clean are my only stipulations," I replied. Just the idea of a burger joint made my stomach turn over.

"Hey man, turn right up ahead! I see something worth checking out!" Steve yelled triumphantly from the back. Damien turned off onto the exit ramp and soon we too could see Steve's restaurant. The building was black, green, and brown. It looked as though it could have been made of old wood. The swirly designs under the paint played out as odd designs against the colors. The black shingle roof bowed at one end which housed a huge black bear eating pancakes as big as its head. The bear was a prop of course, but the pure size of it drew your attention. The parking lot didn't look crowded as we approached but it was lunchtime, and apparently few felt like breakfast. The diner was away from prying eyes and the emptiness only told me there would be no waiting for our food. We could get out of the car, park our butts on non-moving seats for a meal, and be back on the road quickly. Had we known it would be our last decent meal for a long time, and more importantly our last actual bathroom, we would have enjoyed it more.

Damien parked the car and we all climbed out, making a dash for the doors so no one would see us as we crossed the lot. There was no way anyone would know us around here, but we were afraid the trucker could possibly have a great view from the interstate and spot us. Marge didn't maneuver as quickly and was the last one to enter the restaurant. Everyone inside looked the same, as if they had all arrived together, but were in fact road warriors like ourselves. Across from us was the kitchen where you could see the grill and the stainless-steel counter tops. Along the wall hung different nets and fishing gear such as poles and various lures. It was rustic and western but had lots of character.

The boys ordered an unbelievable amount of pancakes. They gobbled them down in some sort of a race. The winning prize was apparently a serious case of indigestion. We ordered coffees to go before the tip was thrown down and then everyone was back outside again. We noticed a group of women standing next to a VW bus. Green and brown swirls covered the entire body of the ride, much like the restaurant it was parked next to. They were dressed in a variety of styles ranging from renaissance fair to punk rock groupie, some with long flowing hair, and one even had a multi-colored Mohawk. When they saw Marge, their faces lit up and they ran towards us with open arms.

"Margie! What the hell happened? We've been so worried!" said an older woman wearing a man's long shirt with a brown vest over it and long pants tucked into cowboy boots. She ran right past the rest of us without a glance and threw her arms around Marge's neck.

"Jesus, don't ever run off on your own like that again!" said another lady slightly younger than the lady before and wearing an equally interesting choice in clothes. Her hair was braided into two separate strands on either side of her head that hung down to her hips. She smelled of old wood when she went past us, and I could see she was wearing sandals with socks. The rest of the women crowded around "Margie" and began talking over one another making the words sound like the cluck of chickens over their feed. Once they were done reuniting, our resident witch turned and introduced us to her crew.

"This, girls, is the kids I went after. The two good looking boys are Damien and Steve. The girl next to Steve there is Sarah, and this, is Josephine." She put her hands on my shoulders and pushed me towards the ladies who all seemed mesmerized to hear my name. Was this the coven? Why, when they heard my name, did they act so dumbfounded? A short lady pushed her way to the front to shake my hand but a shock ran through me as soon as she touched me. It felt like I had shuffled across the carpet and touched the door handle. She slightly shook her hand like she was fanning it and then she spoke.

"Nice to meet you Jo, I'm Marty. Shame about your folks. Good to see you in such great health!" She backed away and went to stand with the other older women who seemed too shy to approach.

"I think we better get going before it gets any later," Marge said to the girls. She gave me a questioning look and I realized she probably didn't want to mention that we were being followed and standing around was not the best strategy. The ladies shook their heads rapidly with a few voicing their agreement and off they went to their van. We continued to stand there, more than a little confused by their sudden appearance.

"We should follow them. They will know the way." Marge replied as she headed to the back of the car and slid in, again, shrouded in mystery. The rest of us slowly shook off the oddness of our situation and headed to the vehicle. What could possibly go wrong? A lot, I suspected.

Chapter Fourteen
THE COVEN OF SECRETS

WE followed the camouflaged van out of town. What an odd-looking bunch they had been. They were nothing like I had expected. How was this hodgepodge group of strange women going to protect us? Cover us in knitted sweaters perhaps, or smooch and pinch the cheeks of our enemies to death? Dye our hair blue and hope we wouldn't be recognized? Some of them might even be old enough to tell us where this ancient enemy came from. The green, brown blur sped up in front of us and turned back towards a south bound lane.

"How did they know where to find us?" I asked towards the backseat.

"The same way we knew what direction to head. Magic comes in handy when used properly," she answered smugly.

"Are you going to teach us about magic?" asked Sarah.

"In time, but I can only teach you the basics. It comes from within you, so only you will know what you're capable of."

"That's awesome!" yelled Steve obviously excited. I was just hoping that once we got there, they didn't feed us to some demigod. I was still on the fence about trusting this lady and her friends with the lives of myself and my family. She had shown some loyalty back there with the semi but she could have just been stalling so her friends could catch up. Unlike Steve, I wasn't ready to be amazed and not suspicious yet. Steve and Sarah were far too trusting. I could tell by the look Damien gave me after

Steve's little outburst, that he was on my side. I smiled at him then turned away towards the van ahead of us.

Why didn't they just tell us where to go? We could be following them anywhere, maybe even to a hair appointment, (which a few of them needed). Without question, we had jumped into our car and followed them. I blamed Marty's words for altering my judgment; they knew about my parents. They were becoming my Achilles's heel. I so desperately wanted to know more about them to find out why I was so special; why I was being hunted. Maybe these senior citizens had just read the paper about the accident and took an interest in the story, and they had nothing new to share with me. For some reason, I didn't feel like that was the case.

Would my parents have been involved with such people? Of course, I didn't really know my parents, so I had no real idea of the type of people they would have known. I tried to picture them in the van ahead of us, swopping stories with a bunch of hippies and Goths.

"Hey, look at that!" Damien yelled from beside me as he pointed out the window towards the woods on the side of the interstate. A buck deer stood proudly amongst the trees, his antlers long and lost among the branches.

"Oh, isn't he lovely!" Sarah said from the backseat as she leaned over the older lady to view the creature from out the window. The deer suddenly ran forward to ram the cars on the highway, only to fall limp to the side of the road ahead of us.

"Oh my God, no!" I couldn't help but yell. The van slowed down in front of us then pulled over to the side where we followed. "What are they doing?" I asked as some of the van doors began to open and a few of the women got out holding jars in their hands.

Marge met our disturbed stares with an unflinching gaze. "Magic is not without a price, children. His death will not be in vain!" She exited the car before any of us could ask another question. Over to the fresh carcass she went where the other ladies were already making busy work with the receptacles. One elder was kneeling beside the creature with her back turned to us handing up jar after jar of some kind of concoction to the ladies around her. They rushed around; trying not to spill the sticky liquid as they screwed on lids then meticulously placed the containers strategically in the van. Jar after jar went until it appeared that the plethora of glass containers had been filled and thoughtfully secured into the bus.

When they all stepped back, bones and other remains of the beast were visible, with blood now running in dark rivulets towards the highway. Marge walked back towards our car, cleaning her hands with a handkerchief from her pocket which she replaced before grabbing the handle. During that brief moment when her hand floated above the door, I thought about locking it. Just the idea of keeping her out and having Damien drive us far away, made me feel more relaxed then if I let that visceral covered woman back into the car to squeeze in with Sarah and Steve. I wanted to leave this mysterious person behind us, along with all the memories of the past two days. No such luck. Marge climbed in beside Steve and Sarah, who no longer looked at her with stars in their eyes. An odor I didn't want to try to describe but I knew was death, filled the cab as a few of us made a mad dash to roll down the windows. I was thankful when we merged back onto the road with a cool breeze of fresh air flowing past, allowing the nasal annoyance to waft right out.

"Oh that feels nice!" Marge exclaimed as she undid her robe and fanned the loose fabric from her sweaty body. "It was so warm out there in all of these clothes."

"Just don't take off anything else." Damien whispered. I nodded in agreement and watched the van before us cut across a lane where it took an exit ramp that read Brevard on its slick green sign.

"Okay, I'll address the pink elephant in the room. What was it you were doing back there?" asked Sarah very professionally.

"A lot of our magic is old and so we do things a little differently than you might expect. Some of our key ingredients come from nature. A recent death of an animal is more powerful than an old one, so we didn't want that magnificent creature to perish there on the side of some highway." She continued to fan herself slightly out of breath.

A gush of air swooshed from Steve and then he said, "I thought that was going to be dinner...boy am I relieved." We all chuckled nervously but I was still curious to know how the remains of the deer could be used in magic. We passed another small sign on the left that read Henderson County. We were still somewhere in Louisiana. I didn't feel any safer. The trucker could be anywhere hiding behind a low billboard or peeking around the wall of a store. My muscles ached from being so tense.

The van ahead of us took the turn and we loyally followed them up the road. From what I could see in all directions there was nothing to write home about, just a few fast-food restaurants and open fields is all I could see. We followed them down another road, away from the little bit of civilization to a tree lined dirt road. The greenery was so thick you couldn't see what lay beyond the walls of vegetation. The van fit in quite nicely with the décor and soon it looked like we were following a dust cloud instead of a vehicle. A clearing opened through the swirling dust as we slowed next to a lone path.

"Is that what I think it is?" Steve questioned aloud as he pointed over the backseat towards the building. There wasn't a sign on the structure indicating what it formerly was but the red and white bricks and slanting roof gave its secret away. Why would an old coven of witches hide out in an abandoned Dairy Queen? The misfortune of the shop was probably due to the distance one would have to travel out of the way for an ice cream cone. Or it could be due to the poor maintenance of the building itself. The parking lot ahead looked like the aftermath of an earthquake with all the odd angles of prutruding cement and huge craters that had been left behind. Our car bounced awkwardly across the uneven surface. We looked like bobble heads as we approached the shack-like structure.

The van parked in the only handicap parking spot that was still visible with distinguishing marks beside the front double doors. Shadows played across the glass. Were there more of them in there or something worse? Once we were parked in the most level spot around, I jumped out and looked around hastily, afraid that I would spot the eighteen-wheeler with the devil for a driver. All I saw was a vast field of emptiness all around us. The building looked sturdy enough for a few more guests. We opened the doors and walked into the dimness inside, noticing the power was off but the witches were being resourceful. The room was illuminated by a variety of sources; candles, oil lamps, skulls with candles in them, and a blue orb in the middle. They were scattered everywhere casting creepy shadows against the glass. Marge went ahead of us and was greeted by the witches that had not been in the van back at the pancake house. Smiles and handshakes greeted us until Marge thought it time for our introductions.

"Girls, these are the kids I went after. Here is Steven and his lovely lady friend Sarah." She pushed both Steve and Sarah in front of her and the ladies made a circle around them. "Sarah has the 'touch' and I think Steve will come into his own very soon." New smiles were on their faces as they thrust their hands forward or reached up and hugged the two new members. Then it was our turn, and the ladies parted allowing Steve and Sarah to move to the back of the restaurant and take a seat in an empty booth. Damien took my hand and proceeded forward. I appreciated the comfort of his touch as we reached the center of the circle. The possibly twenty-some odd ladies stepped back and allowed more room for Damien's big build. I could feel a warm embrace inside the circle. Maybe that was why Sarah and Steve looked so at ease when they had entered.

"This large man before us is Damien." She patted his bulging triceps for emphasis. "He is training with dark energy, and I must say he is coming along very nicely." She winked at Damien as the first of many hands was thrust for a shake and names were given. Some of the ladies barely came up to Damien's chest but he accommodated them well and leaned down so they could give him a hug. Many of them smiled and there was hushed, excited whispers in the air. Finally, all the women had introduced themselves to Damien and I stared at my feet knowing it was my turn.

"This charming child is Josephine Kelley, who I'm sure you might remember. She's a ghost walker but I believe there is more within just waiting to burst out!" She slapped me on the back which sent me into the arms of the lady in front of me who looked down with a big toothy smile. The room went black all around me as everyone crowded around, blocking out the light. Some were touching my face, others trying to hug me. Their names fell on deaf ears as the room seemed to roar with voices. The air was warm as many faces rotated around me, limiting my oxygen. I felt a nudge and Damien pulled me beside him, once more my rock I could lean on since my legs were about to give out. He felt me weave next to him and he placed his arm around me to steady me on my feet. I felt like I had just been beaten by the paparazzi! Everyone had wanted a piece of me, an arm or a leg if they could get it, just to say hi? What was I, a savior to them or something?

"Ladies, now no need to go scaring the child half to death! Give her some breathing room!" Marge came to stand in front of us like a shield, waving her arms about like she was fanning flies. "Back now, back," she shooed as the circle around us dispersed, and the ladies spread as thin as the eatery would allow. I was thankful for the space, and I took a deep breath of the empty air before I felt solid again.

"So sorry. We had just heard so much about you and were anxious to meet ya," said a round, overweight woman from far off to the right. More murmurs of apology went out through the room as Marge turned to me.

"There are a few things I have yet to tell you, dear. One of the important ones being the relationship we had with your mother...She was one of us, at one time, back before she met your father. We all had some good times back then." Her eyes seemed to glaze over as she was reminiscing. She shook her head. "The resemblance is striking." Some of the women wiped their eyes as others cleared their throats. My mother had been one of them here in the run down DQ? I couldn't picture her amongst people who used dead animals for strange primitive type rituals. Could she have been the one on her knees scooping gore into a jar and handing it off down the assembly line?

I just couldn't imagine her like that; not even when I closed my eyes and wished she would come and tell me it was a lie. My parents had been normal and so was I until their tragic passing, or so I had thought. What if she was telling the truth, though?

"Susan, no need in doing that. She will come around on her own." Margie looked sternly at an old black lady who had been standing next to me. How was it that I didn't hear her approach? "She didn't mean any harm; she has the power of persuasion, and she just wanted to help you come to terms with this new information." The lady stepped back bowing her head as she merged amongst the other faces in the crowd. "Now where was I? Oh yes! Your mother had an unusual gift for a ghost walker. It almost bordered necromancy, but she didn't raise the dead." She took a pause and I used the moment of silence to swallow the information. A person could choke trying to take so much in at once but I took a deep breath and gestured to her to finish.

"She started off like you, only able to speak to the dead when they approached her, but later she learned how to evoke the spirits of the dead to come to her. She was practicing the art of containing them, just the evil ones, whenever she was killed. You can make a lot of enemies with that kind of power. When we tried to warn her, we were blocked by dark forces," she paused to gain her composure. "The paper was a horrible way to find out they had passed but..." She began to choke on a sob and another member came forward to finish her tell.

"We saw you had survived, and we made arrangements to come and get you. Every time we got close, the evil ones would come. They were using us to try and find you. We were once 35 combined members but now we're down to 20 after our last battle. We thought we could fight the evil ourselves; that was a lesson we had to learn...from experience." She took a moment to mourn her fallen friends, then shook her head and placed a comforting hand on Marge's shoulder. The multi-colored mohawk woman moved to the front to finish.

"We can protect ourselves better now than we could before. Which is why we felt it was time to come and get you. We found out you were leaving our circle of protection to go to Mississippi, so Marge sent her spirit guide to warn you. Unfortunately, you had lost your ability to hear the dead and she was unable to stop you. When she failed to warn you again with the writing, Margie left to find you on her own." She turned to the others who all nodded their heads in agreement while I just stood there, crushed by a tidal wave of information that had yet to completely settle in. My mom had been one of them at one time, but I was no one to them. Why was I so important to these people that they would risk their lives, just to protect me? Still, I was missing a bigger picture; the lady I had thought could be my enemy, was actually the one who had been protecting me all along.

"I'm sure my mother truly appreciates everything you have sacrificed for my protection. Sorry I caused you all so much trouble, and I hope there is a way I can repay you when this is all over." I felt humbled by this. Most of my life I had struggled for love and acceptance, and just to understand my place in the world. But these women, strangers to me, were willing to give up everything! Damien gave me a squeeze of reassurance. I felt at ease, for once, in Damien's embrace, amongst people who treated me like family. Perhaps we could be truly safe here. I had been searching for so long for answers. Maybe I had found home at last?

Chapter Fifteen
FAMILY

"OKAY girls, let's quit standing around with stupid grins on our faces," said a tall lanky lady wiping a tear from her eye. "We've got loads to do!" Instantly, the room was filled with commotion as the ladies ran around banging pots and pans together in the kitchen while others were bringing in wood that had been stacked up outside.

"Can we help?" Damien asked one of the ladies as she passed.

"You boys need to pull the cars around back. There's a camouflage tarp you can throw over your ride next to the dumpsters." She tossed them keys that had a peace symbol dangling from it. The boys shot out of the restaurant towards the vehicles, eager to help, and I headed to the booth in the back where Sarah was still sitting.

"It's so nice, what they're doing for us. I just knew, right away, it was a good idea to come here. It just felt right, you know?" she said.

"I just hope the cost in helping me won't be high." I thought about all the souls they had lost already. What if they all died for nothing? What if I couldn't stop what's coming? "What if I get these powers and turn evil or something?" I said accidently aloud.

"Jo, you know you could never be evil. You've never even cheated on a test, besides, it's just not in your blood to be a bad person." Sarah comforted.

"My mom was trying to contain dead spirits! Dead people. What good could have come from that?" I asked, not seeing the potential in something so heinous.

"I don't know, maybe she was helping people get rid of poltergeists or something. Aren't they supposed to be demons? Or how about people possessed?" she perked up, eyes wide. "I've seen plenty of movies with exorcisms and they don't look easy. Your mom could just walk into the room and say, 'get in my jar,' or something cool like that and then poof, done. That sounds like a good and helpful thing to me." She rested her hand on my shoulder, and I bowed my head. She was right, I could never be evil and my mom had to have a good reason for wanting to practice such an ability. It all made sense; however, it didn't make me feel better. "Come on sour puss, there's bound to be something we can do to take your mind off things. We could set the table or something, 'kay?"

Plates and silverware were clanking in the kitchen area and a nice aroma was filling the eatery. The boys had finished their first duty and now they were helping rearrange the dining room to accommodate us all in one big row. Sarah and I headed to the counter to see if we could help out.

"Is there anything we can do?" Sarah asked the heavy set woman carrying more wood into the kitchen.

"I'm sure the girls could use you, Sarah, as they cast the protection spell. Here, come with me and I'll show you." She laid her load on the floor and grabbed Sarah's arm, leaving me alone amongst the bustling women. I spotted Marge reading the labels of a variety of seasonings and I thought maybe she could give me a job as well.

"Hey, I'm not much of a cook but I'm sure there's something I can help you with," I said with a smile.

"I think we're all out of basil, but there is more out back in the green house. Why don't you go fetch some?" She smiled at me and patted my back while I headed for the exit. The sun had started its descent over the mountains and the sky was awash with different shades of purple and pink. I went around to the side of the building but what I saw, I had not expected. The enclosure that surrounded the dumpster typically had been removed and covered in green plastic. After entering the tent, I noticed nice, neat shelves that had pots on them, well organized with little pictures and the name of each item. I easily found the basil, but I had forgotten to ask how much to bring, so I grabbed the pot and brought the whole thing with me. I could hear the hum of women's voices in the air as I walked back to the entrance of the building. I followed the sound to see what Sarah was doing to help and what a protective spell entailed when I noticed an aroma in the air. I lifted the pot up to my nose to see if the basil was making the elusive scent but all I could smell was wet dirt and a sweet stench coming from the plant. I saw a circle of women and I snuck closer to get a better view of the ceremony. Their backs were turned towards me with a steaming kettle in the center. Sarah was pacing around the circle with smoking twigs in her hand that was causing a smell of sage to be released into the air. The smell was inviting but when I got closer to the ring, I felt an invisible wall. The force was see-through to the eye but it stung when I touched it. I didn't try to place my hand through it, I had a bad feeling that something not-so-good would happen. The smoke seemed to completely engulf the women as their heads fell back and they moaned towards the sky.

"Freaky," I said out loud as I took a step back from the circle and headed to the hideout. They were definitely going to show me how to do that, right? It would come in handy with ex-boyfriends, bill collectors, and the occasional out-door barbeque. Back inside the sanity of the building, I approached the counter and laid down the pot I had left to retrieve.

"Got the herb here. Maybe you could give me a little insight into what the ladies are doing out there, huh?" I asked Marge while leaning in, in case it was a secret.

"I'm sure there will be plenty of time once dinner is over and we're making the sleeping arrangements. Here, take these and set the tables the boys fixed up." She handed me a stack of plates and forks which she topped with old yellowed Dairy Queen napkins. I huffed; should have figured she'd blow me off again. I walked over to the makeshift dining table and marveled over the excellent job the boys had done with the combinations of tables and booths. Instead of individual tables, there was now one long one down the middle of the dining room on which I placed the dinner utensils. Chairs lined either side of the table ending with a stool on either end. The candles made a nice center piece in the middle of the set-up but the smell of the food to come was far more pleasing.

"Soups on, girls!" a burley woman with short hair yelled to the witches outside. It didn't take long before we were all seated, filling the former restaurant with sounds of scraping chairs and conversation. The mush of meat and vegetables in front of me was delicious but I was more enthused with the conversation around me.

"Has anyone heard from Bertie?" Marge asked a skinny lady with long dark hair.

"No, but she's bound to return soon with the package. She left on the Ruckus shortly after you arrived," she answered.

"What package?" asked Sarah because she was closer to the conversation then I was.

"It's just something to help Jo develop a little faster. We're kind of crunched on time and this will give her a boost," replied Marge, quickly glancing around the room, daring anyone to say more on the matter. What could they possibly be planning now?

"Is there something I can take that will help me be more efficient?" Sarah, always trying to be at her best but I still felt betrayed with her quick interrogation with these people. I knew she wasn't trying to hurt me and her friendliness was just a show of her character. Her new ability would at least keep her at a distance from our enemies, plus it gave her the advantage of knowing their location. As long as she would be kept safe, the rest just felt like a bonus.

"Sam is going to be training you to help you expand your talent. She has a lot of experience in the limitations of the human psyche." A nice-looking Asian lady sitting further down from Sarah bowed to her and Sarah awkwardly bowed back and smiled. She looked to be slightly shorter than Sarah and her hair had yet to lose its dark brown color although frown lines outlined her lips revealing she was older. I wondered what Sam was short for and I opened my mouth to ask but I was interrupted.

"We still don't know much about you, Marge. What do you do?" asked Steve. That was a better question then what I had so I shut my mouth and took another bite of meat.

"I'm a guardian. I watch out for power shifts within our plane of existence, I keep in constant contact with the spirit world, and I protect others like us. I'm a pretty good cook too!" She took another sip of her soup while I tried to swallow this information. I had already witnessed a few of the talents she had listed and none of them seemed similar to my own.

I wondered if Bertie, and what she brings, would help me in my training. It would be added to the outstanding list of questions I had already compiled for after dinner conversation. The rest of the meal was rather uneventful and ended with me and the skinny dark-haired lady doing the dishes. I took the opportunity to ask a few of the questions I had to the lady who called herself Crystal.

"How long have you been with this coven?" I asked, trying to start with the easy questions first.

"Since I was about your age," she said not giving anything away as she handed me a warm, soapy plate. By looking at her, I couldn't tell how old she was per se, but I had a guess that she was around forty. Maybe I could buddy up with this lady and get more info from her that way.

"So you joined, what, eight years ago?" A little flattery goes a long way.

"That won't get you anywhere. Why don't you just ask me, flat out, what you want without this pussy-footing around?" She slopped another sudsy bowl my way and I rinsed it off slowly before I responded. Great, straight to the point.

"I don't think I've met Bertie yet. Some of the others were talking about her at dinner. Is she sick or something?" I probed.

"I know you must have overheard that she made a little trip to find something useful for your training or you wouldn't be asking." Wow, I was liking this Crystal gal.

"I'll admit I overheard but I didn't mean to eavesdrop. Is it true that it will help me develop faster?" I asked while stacking the dry dishes on the shelf with the others.

"If we can convince *it* to join us, *it* would be very valuable. Now, no more questions till you've spoken to Marge, okay? She has more answers than I do," she said sternly as she laid another soapy bowl into my hand. What did she mean by convince *it*? Was this some kind of new magic they planned on using on me or what? If only she hadn't shut me out so I could ask her more questions. The rest of our chore went quickly and once all the dishes were stacked back in their cupboards, I met up with Sarah and the boys at the car to discuss what new info I had in private.

"Why help us to strengthen our abilities and not give us any answers? I just don't know if I can trust these people," Damien stated as he put his arm around my shoulders while Steve passed out bottled waters from the cooler in our trunk.

"I think they're nice," Sarah replied after taking a big gulp.

"Yes, but you think everyone is nice. I suspect your opinion is a little biased, after all, Marge showed you how to do your radar power. That kind of makes her like your sensei or something." Sarah lightly punched Steve on the arm in response to his comment but it was very true.

"I think we should be careful. None of us go off with them alone. Not until we know more or why their being so secretive. We stay in pairs until we get this thing figured out, okay?" Damien requested.

"They're just a bunch of nice old ladies, they couldn't hurt a fly." Steve replied with a flick of his wrist.

"Chauvinist!" Sarah said angrily with a light slap to the back of Steve's head. "I bet if they were a bunch of dudes you wouldn't think that!"

"Don't be naive man, I think we should be careful, that's all." Damien said levelly.

"I think that's smart," I agreed, hugging him with one arm. A yawn escaped and I stretched my arms out with it. "Now let's go see where we'll be sleeping tonight." We walked back around to the front of the restaurant where small tents had been pitched in the grass. We had not come prepared to spend the night under the stars since we thought we would be in hotel rooms for most of our trip. I didn't want to think about how closely I might have to snuggle with total strangers. One of the witches stepped out the front doors and motioned to the boys to come back into the restaurant, leaving Sarah and I to help the ladies fan out the dusty blankets.

"Here, grab this end," I motioned to Sarah. We shook the old blanket out and watched the ancient dust particles fly off into the air.

"I can do this by myself, why don't you go over there and talk to Marge. I'm sure she would be happy to answer those questions you had. I can watch you from here." She winked and motioned to the witch over by the greenhouse filling a watering can. I headed towards the shack to finally get some of my questions answered.

"Hey there, can I help?" I asked question number one.

"Sure, grab those pots." She pointed to some empty pots on the ground next to the make-shift greenhouse. I packed them with me into the small enclosure behind her. I had already gone against Damien's wishes but they knew where I was in case they needed to find my body. Suddenly all the instruments on the shelves looked like weapons. "So I'm sure you didn't just come in here to help with the gardening. Go ahead, ask me." Maybe Marge had psychic powers as well.

"I don't know where to start." I stated quit honestly. "How about the story of how you knew my parents?"

"Well, your mother was a sweet child, always playing in the dirt and messing up her clothes. She didn't change much when she grew up. She was still kind and not afraid to get her hands dirty." She shook her head back and forth chuckling to herself at the memories. "When she met your dad, the whole world stopped. Instantly, he was her everything and I protested when she said she wanted to get married at eighteen years of age. We all agreed that they were rushing into things. He was her first real boyfriend and her whole life was ahead of her. He was a biker and that didn't help matters any. He turned out to be a good kid though, very courteous."

"My Dad was a biker?" I said surprised.

"Oh, yes, and then you came along, and he gave it up to be a family. We didn't see them much after that, they thought this kind of life was just too dangerous for a baby, but they brought you on visits just the same. It broke the girls' hearts when I decided to stop them from trying to retrieve you after so many failed attempts." She pulled a herb out of a pot and fiddled with its roots trying to separate it into two sprigs.

"Why did you feel you needed to make that decision?" I asked wondering who put her in charge of my life.

"You were going to find out one way or another so here goes kiddo," she took a deep breath. "I'm your grandmother." She put down everything in her hands and gave me her full attention to review my reaction. I didn't stick around to hear what she had to say next. All the oxygen had left the tiny greenhouse and I had to rush outside to take a breath of fresh air and collect my thoughts. Deep down, I felt like maybe I had known all along. Could it have just been some kind of expression like she felt like she was my grandmother due to her long close relationship with my mother? There had to be a way to find out if this woman was truly crazy or if she was telling the truth. I just couldn't wrap my head around it. I walked out into the field, thinking that if only I could have a moment to be alone, I might be able to find and talk to my parents again and get confirmation. They wouldn't lie to me and there were other answers that were long overdue. Mostly, I just wanted to yell at someone for not telling me sooner.

"Hey, Jo, wait up!" Damien yelled jogging up beside me. "Sarah said you went to talk to Marge. What happened?" I was too overwhelmed to answer so I kept walking. "Jo? Babe, stop for a minute!" He grabbed my arm and spun me around to look at him.

"She told me she is my Grandmother, okay? I just need a minute." I didn't want to yell at him, but he had stopped me, and my emotions were still high. I could see him taking in this new pile of dung I had just thrown at him, and it caused him to momentarily stop in his tracks. I could tell the wheels were turning in his head and I appreciated the silence so I could collect myself. I began walking again, determined that I was going to figure this out.

"Jo, it doesn't change anything," he yelled after me. "Where are you going? There's no reason for you to leave on foot when we've got a car!" He caught up to me again.

"I'm not going anywhere!" I threw my arms up in defeat. "I just need to be alone, so I can try and contact my parents again. I just can't believe this; I have to know for sure." He grabbed my arm gently again and stopped me in mid-stride.

"So do your thing, but I'm going to be right here waiting and watching out for you. I'm not going to leave you alone, Jo.

Never." He pulled me into a hug and lightly squeezed. I'm now angry at myself. There was no reason for me to let loose on him like that when he wasn't the one I was mad at. I lightly kissed him, and he released me from his comforting embrace.

"I'm sorry. I just need a minute to meditate, cool down. All this stress is just a bit overpowering right now." He nodded understandingly as I slowly walked away from him, indicating a spot in the short distance that I was heading to. We had already gotten far enough away from the buildings that I felt things would be quiet enough. I flopped down on the grass and Damien kept his distance. I appreciated not having the distraction. The sun was almost completely gone behind the mountain as the night-time insects started making their music. I took some deep breaths and grounded myself, paying attention to the feeling of the breeze on my skin and the aroma of damp grass. I tried to be calm, at peace, but I had so many questions that it made it difficult to clear my mind. I tried again, pushing past all the darkness, trying to see the bright light of my secret place. A pinhole of light appeared in the distance. It grew bigger gradually as I relaxed, knowing that everything was about to be answered.

I opened my eyes, and I was standing in a grove where oranges and pears trees glistened in the sunlight. Their shades of pale green and orange were bright against the blue clear sky. The babbling brook flowed gracefully past me, and birds tweeted as they flew overhead. I was completely at ease here, but I didn't see anyone else. I felt discouraged and walked towards the first tree ahead of me, hoping to find them behind it. Still nothing. Only more trees and emptiness. I sat down under the small tree and leaned my back against the sturdy bark. Where were they or better yet, where could they have gone? I hit my head against the tree in frustration. Tapping on my shoulder startled me and I threw my body forward and turned around still on my knees.

"What the hell..." I started but then I saw my dad's smiling face amongst the tree branches. "What are you doing in the tree?" I asked, getting to my feet and dusting the dirt from my knees.

"I'm hiding! We didn't want 'it' finding us. Your mother's gone off to try and divert 'it' away from here, so we would have a chance to talk."

"You let mom go alone?" I couldn't believe my Dad would allow my Mother to be put in harm's way while he hid, and I let the disappointment show in my tone.

"We knew you would be coming back so one of us had to stay. I'm no match for 'him' but your Mom can give 'him' a run for his money. The tree seemed like a comfortable place to wait," Dad answered.

"Well, you scared the bejesus out of me, Dad! How did you know I would be back?" I questioned.

"We're family hun; we watch over you all the time. We figured it wouldn't be long before you had a question or two about what's going on out there."

"Well, you're right, I need to know Dad, is Marge really my grandmother?"

"Sorry to say the crazy old bag, who never liked me by the way, really is your grandmother. On your mother's side, mind you. You can trust her. I wish we could have told you earlier but there wasn't time." He jumped down from the tree and landed on his feet next to me.

"I don't think my head can handle any more surprises! It's all just too much to take in at once. Why is this *all* happening now, it's too much." He patted my shoulder sympathetically.

"You're older, honey, you've gotten stronger and the evil senses that. They're afraid you will be powerful like your mom and they know they can't control you. You're a special case you know, the only one left with the potential to stop what's coming."

"These powers don't make me any more special than Marge or any of the other ladies of the coven." A cloud passed before the sun and everything became covered in shade.

"You can walk in both worlds. That's something that no one at your grandmother's coven can do. Now, I know you have more questions but...they're coming." The darkness seemed to grow thicker with his words. "You have to go!" He shoved me lightly in the direction I had originally came from and I turned my worried face back to him. "Don't look at me like that, we'll be fine, we're already dead." He kissed me on the forehead. "Remember, we love you." I felt tears starting to form in my eyes.

"I'll be back! Take care of mom!" I shouted behind me, and everything went black. I opened my eyes one at a time and found myself in the dark amongst tall grass.

"Damien!" I shouted making sure I was in the field outside the restaurant once again.

"I'm here," he said coming towards me. "Is everything okay?" I blew out a relieved sigh.

"I'm fine. I just wanted to make sure you were still there."

"I wouldn't leave you. Were you able to see them?" He took a seat next to me.

"Yes. Let's just sit here for a few more minutes, okay? Let me catch my breath." He placed a comforting arm around my shoulders. We stayed like that for a long while, sitting in the tall grass, just the two of us, watching over the women's camp below. "My dad confirmed it, I officially have a crazy witch for a grandmother." I laughed out loud hearing the words. He gave me a squeeze.

"So what do you feel like doing now? I don't want to make any decisions going forward without knowing if you're going to be okay." He took my hand and kissed it while looking in my eyes. I thought over his question in my head.

"Honestly, I just want to get some sleep and I know everyone probably feels the same. After a good night's rest, we can all talk about a plan of action. I just feel like I have brain fog and I can't be trusted to make good decisions when I feel like that." I got up to my knees and smiled at him. He smiled back and stood up, extending his arm out to me to help me up.

We talked briefly about the different ladies we had met as a distraction as we headed back. I wanted to ask him about his power which I didn't know anything about, but I'd had enough information for one night. We had waited this long to talk about it, what was another night? I felt that when he was ready, he would talk, and I needed to trust that he knew what he was doing. I didn't know how much time had passed since we had walked up the hill and now down it hand in hand, but it felt late. Marge was there waiting at the front door for me.

"So, did you get the confirmation you needed?" she asked with her arms across her chest. No surprise she knew what I had just done but I wouldn't play her games right now. I nodded to her as I fanned away a yawn. I needed to reboot; tomorrow would be another day filled with unanswered questions. I walked past her into the hideout where Steve and Sarah were fast asleep in a booth. Damien and I grabbed a few of the blankets that were folded on a table and headed to the back booth that would serve as our bed for the evening. The old lady stuck her head in and said, "we'll be changing out the guard ever so often so don't be surprised when one of us comes to wake you for a shift change." Her head disappeared and left only silence behind as Damien and I tried squeezing into a booth where we could sleep opposite one another.

"I love you, Jo," he said reaching out his hand to me.

"I love you, too," I responded while taking his hand. That was the last thing I heard before I yielded to sleep and they were the best ones.

Chapter Sixteen

GETTING TO KNOW GRAM

THE next day I awoke alone in my booth. Once I was fully alert and realized I was alone, I panicked, but Sarah was by me in a flash.

"Jo, you're okay. We're in an old restaurant." Like that was comforting.

"Where's Damien?" I asked my voice still gravelly from sleep.

"He and Steve are on morning patrol while the ladies fix breakfast. I told them we could have the cereal out in our car, but they insisted on fixing us some big banquet. They said we needed our strength," Sarah finished, looking much too perky.

"What for?" I asked stupidly, still shaking off the remnants of a nightmare.

"For training of course! I'm so excited I could hardly wait until you woke up to tell you!" She was already dressed in fresh clothes, ready for another dramatic day. I felt like lying there, wishing I could sleep forever. I was reminded of a thought: didn't I have to wait until Bertie came back to train me? What was the hurry? I got up and stretched the kinks out of my back from the uncomfortable booth before I reluctantly stumbled to the bathroom to change clothes. I would have felt better if I could have had a shower but the sink, which didn't even have enough pressure for a good spit bath, would have to do.

I couldn't imagine how the old ladies had managed to find such a rundown shack to live in. Hopefully, last night would be the first and last time I would ever sleep in a booth again. I splashed the lukewarm water on my face and dried it with a brown paper towel. I changed into some comfortable tan shorts with a dark tank in case I too would play in the dirt today as my mother did so many years ago. I could hear the dining room booming with people before I walked out. The noise was loud and would have woken me had Sarah waited. I headed to the tables that had been reassembled for breakfast and I strolled over to an empty seat next to Sarah. Shortly after that, the guys joined us. Breakfast was filling and the chores afterward were uneventful. It seemed like none of the witches were talking and yet the seamless chatter never stopped. Even more stressful was the fact that I had yet to see this 'Bertie' anywhere. Maybe I was just to learn the basics today and learn the hard stuff when she got back?

Sarah and Steve met up with Sam, the Asian lady, and I waited to see who would be taking me. Damien went off with the burley lady in men's clothing who we had met outside the pancake house. It turned out her name was Lillie, which was more of a delicate name than I would have pictured for her. As he walked away, he looked over his shoulder, afraid to leave me alone but I waved at him to signify that I would be fine. There was no reason for me to fear being alone with these women anymore. Everyone disappeared into the tall grass fields as I stood alone, leaning against the wall of the restaurant, and squinting into the early morning light as it started its adventure across the sky.

"Hey kiddo," came a noise beside me. I knew her voice by now and I didn't turn to meet her gaze.

"What do you want now? You have more life changing things to *share* with me?" Some of my anger was grumpiness from lack of sleep but the rest was all for her.

"I know you're angry with me, but you have to believe that everything I did, I did because I care about you. That being said, how about we start your training?" She walked away from me and headed to the forest beyond the eatery. I didn't want to follow her at first, but I knew it was just me being a stubborn child, so I took off behind my recently acquainted Grandmother. I'm sure it's best for both of us if I quit playing the blame game with her and just accept it. After all, she was all the family I had left.

"So, what are we going to do that requires being amongst so many trees?" I couldn't imagine learning any new moves or practicing my new skills in a space that barely provided room for our two forms.

"We are going to learn to listen today," she said, sitting down under a tree in the lotus yoga position. I was surprised I didn't hear things besides the forest floor popping and cracking as she made it down without assistance. I followed suit as we both sat in silence for what seemed like ages until finally, I couldn't stand it any longer.

"Why did you wait to tell me? Why not announce yourself right away instead of dragging me all this way to tell me?" I asked.

"There were bigger things going on that had to be dealt with before we could have our time. I wanted to wait until we were in a safe place to have this discussion," she replied keeping her eyes closed and her hands out in front of her knees.

"Well, here we are! You've got me in a position where I have nowhere else to go, so it's not like I can just run away. Was that your plan all along?" I didn't like confessing my vulnerability to this woman, but she made me feel so openly angry.

"There's no reason to get so defensive, child. I've only thought about you every moment since you all left us that terrible night. Your wellbeing is priority number one for me and my girls. The best we could do was call in a favor to a fine lady that fosters a lot of kids." I thought about this for a moment while staring at her emotionless face.

"You mean Mamma D?" I asked surprised.

"How'd you think you got so lucky to be put in such a healing place after all the bad homes you had seen?" She stared at me with her hands now moved to her hips like she was waiting for an answer. "Didn't take much pushing. She's always eager to help kids, and without any magical abilities of her own making her a target, you were well hidden." I sat back against the tree and meditated on the thought of Momma D and my grandmother knowing one another. I just couldn't picture it, but I didn't want to be the one to look a gift horse in the mouth. My foster life was good because of her and the other kids. Without them, I might not have turned out as good as I did.

"I know I should be thanking you for everything, but it's still hard for me to do. I'm not sure if having things turn out differently would have changed me but I *was* kept safe, for the most part. I have you to thank for that...so thanks, I guess." I struggled to spit the words out.

"You're welcome, kiddo. Now let's be completely open with each other from here on out, okay?" She moved her hand to my arm and lightly patted it.

"Sure, I can do that, but what should I call you?" I ran through the list of things I had already been calling her in my head and decided that none of them were appropriate.

"I've always liked Gram. Doesn't make me sound too old or nothing." I rolled the name over in my head.

"Okay, *Gram*," it came out sounding sarcastic, "now that we have that out of the way, why did I have to be hidden? What makes me any more special then all of you?"

"Do you remember anything, before the accident?" she asked.

"Do you mean if I remember you? I barely recall my parents by feelings and smells. Until recently, I only had their pictures to remind me of what they looked like."

"Why only recently?" she continued her interrogation.

"Because they just now came to me, to warn me of something coming. Why is it that after all these years, I finally see them now?" I questioned.

"I'm sure you haven't heard this enough yet but you're getting stronger. I wasn't sure you'd see my spirit guide's warnings, but it turns out you had only lost your ability to hear the dead. Were you able to hear your parents before?"

"No, but when I *do* see them, it's not the same as when I see dead people in general. It's different with them." My legs were starting to ache from the prolonged state of being in the same position. I stretched them out in front of me and wiggled them a little to get the feeling back.

"How's it different, Jo? Try describing it to me." She turned so she could look me in the face as I answered.

"I like to go to a peaceful place in my head to relax. I had all these reports to write and research to do that just was too much, so I got into yoga to calm myself and de-stress my mind.

When I got centered and found my usual spot, I found I wasn't alone. That's when they came to me, during my meditation, and told me about the danger coming. Well, a little about it, anyway." I felt myself shifting under her gaze.

"I see..." she said drifting off in thought.

"What? You said we would be open with one another. You obviously know something," I stated with a furrowed brow.

"Jo, you've been repressing your abilities for years. It was this stress that interfered with it, which is why your parents came to you at last. In your moment of absolute need. Once your abilities were turned up, you were like a beacon to me...and to the Trickster."

"So how do I turn it back off and make him go away?" I asked eagerly.

Marge shook her head sadly, "Oh, honey! It doesn't work that way. The universe knows you now, and it won't let you go." That sounded ominous.

"So, you're saying that I've suddenly started broadcasting to the entire universe? 'Hey, universe, it's me, Jo!' Come one, come all and kill me!" I might have been yelling but we were in the woods for a reason.

"There's no way to know for sure. It does explain why the wheels are in motion now. There's only a handful of us that have been able to do what you just described, and even fewer of them are still alive." She rested her chin in her hand, and she looked to be considering what to do with me.

"You know it really isn't that different then seeing the dead when my eyes are open. I don't think it's some new special thing at all." I tried to brush it off and make our situation more manageable, but I was failing. "Should I stop doing it?" I asked after some thought.

"What you are seeing is those that have passed over, and those that have yet to be judged. It's rare to see them and even rarer when you don't know what to look for." She seemed excited for me, but I felt a ball of dread deep within myself. Just another thing that made me a freak I guess, what was the harm in that?

"Can Bertie, do it? Is that why I'm waiting to train when she gets back?" I asked.

"No, Bertie doesn't know how to see the dead at all. Her special skill is tracking which is what she's doing right now. She is tracking something down for us that will help in your training." Still with the secrecy.

"What is she bringing back?" I asked, starting to become more uncomfortable on the harsh under brush.

"We'll deal with that when it gets here. No need in getting you all excited so you're disappointed if she shows up empty-handed. I must ask though, what's it look like, where your parents are?"

"Don't you know?" I asked her.

"You think I'm that good? Lordy, no! I've only heard about it, but I don't have the skill to actually go there." She chuckled at me like something was funny. I wanted to ask where 'there' was exactly, but I decided to just answer her question and find out later.

"It's a vast, endless space that's beautiful hues of blues and greens. There's a clear stream and an orchard full of assorted fruits. It seems peaceful there for the most part. Does this place have a name?"

"Think of it as God's waiting room for those coming and going; some waiting to be judged, others waiting to see their loved ones. Don't worry, it's not Purgatory. Not everyone goes to Heaven either, but that doesn't mean you don't want to see them once more before they're cast down."

"So it's like a dorm lounge for the dead to meet up in? Like we have at school."

"Yes, something like that. I have never heard of anyone getting to stay there for long periods of time but it's how most psychics communicate with those that have passed over. Are your parents always there when you go?" Gram quizzed me further.

"Yes, but last time Dad said he was hiding so 'they' wouldn't find him while Mom was away. Sometimes when I'm there, it gets dark, and my parents said 'they' were coming but they never elaborated on who 'they' were. Do you know? Is it the same evil that's after me?" Finally, I was getting some answers to the questions I had been carrying around all this time and I could literally feel weight being lifted from my shoulders.

"I think that even in death, the evil ones are still trying to claim you and your parents. Your mother is clever, so I know she'll continue to fight 'them' off and buy us more time. I just hope that Bertie gets back, that way-" We were interrupted by the sounds of small engines approaching. We emerged from the woods overlooking the parking lot where a scooter and a motorcycle had just arrived.

"Is that Bertie down there?" I asked her.

"It appears that her mission was successful. Let's go down and meet your aunt, shall we?"

Chapter Seventeen
BREAKING NEW GROUND

AN aunt? I had *more* family to meet. The air around me felt thick and made it hard to breathe as I descended the hill. I saw the familiar dark hair of a younger lady who then turned to look up at us as we made our way down. It made me stop. She had my mother's face and I stood frozen holding my breath. I just didn't think I had it in me to go down and meet her.

"Come on dear, she won't bite." Gram said as she stopped and turned back to look at me.

"How do I know that? I've never even heard of her before now," I protested. Not one picture, not one mention of this mysterious creature before me, till now.

"That's ridiculous, she's family!" she replied as she continued walking down the hill towards the crowd that had started to form around the new arrivals. I really didn't believe she would bite, but I didn't want to go down there and play nice with someone whose very face made my heart ache. How dare she look so much like my mother without being her? What kind of cruel joke was it to spring something like this on me? A moment to prepare was needed and deserved. I stood lifeless halfway down the hill, afraid to move forward and contemplating hiding in the woods.

Movement from the field below caught my attention. I saw my friends going to meet the stranger that I was afraid to meet. I had already met so many in such a short period of time and this one was family (which was become not as rare as it used to be). I wasn't a coward so why was this one person so intimidating to me? I took a deep breath and put a smile on my face as I headed down to the parking lot where my Gram was introducing her living daughter to those who had yet to meet her. Damien was by my side again and I was grateful. The strain would break me at any moment and push me to tears if I were alone. I came to the conclusion that since my new life was *full* of surprises, and heightened moments of *stress*, I would just let them roll off my back, rather than swoosh me. I approached my new Aunt and thrusted out my hand in greeting. She looked at it awkwardly for a minute before she reached out and hugged me.

"I didn't know, I'm sorry! I would have come and got you right away if I'd known you were in danger!" She looked over at Gram and gave her a dirty look that said a lot about their relationship. She held me tightly towards her chest again like she was protecting me from the old ladies, and I finally had to pull out of her grip to breathe.

"Nice to meet you," I gasped. OMG, was this one crazy as well?

"We tried to get a hold of you but it's not like you left contact information behind. If it wasn't for Bertie here, we would have never found you!" Gram said defensively in response to the stranger.

"If I'd wanted to be found, you would have found me without the need for Beatrice here." She pointed her thumb towards the bulky woman who was frowning back at her for having her first name used. I think I liked Bertie better too, but I was more concerned about what the argument between my aunt and Grandmother was about. What happened amongst them that couldn't be resolved quickly and quietly instead of being a big production in front of us all?

"Well, I think it's time for us to prepare lunch. I'm sure the ladies will whip something fancy up for an old friend." Gram smiled and turned on her heel as the rest of the ladies silently went into the complex, leaving us to stand with the new arrival.

"So you're Jo's aunt, uh?" asked Sarah approaching the lady with her arms open as if to say she was unarmed but in truth I think she was feeling the power roll off her as I did.

I didn't know if it was all the witches, but now that they're gone, the one left in front of us was giving off some seriously ticked off, 'don't mess with me or you'll regret it', vibes.

"Yeah...sorry about that; bad blood. Anyhow, I'm Dawn. You are?" she asked,

the massive barrier around her slowly receding back as Sarah and I gradually approached.

"I'm Sarah, Jo's best friend. This is my sweetie Steve and his brother Damien. He's also Jo's fiancé." It had been so long since I heard that word that I had to turn and look at Damien beside me and grin.

"He's cute," she said as she adjusted the pack on her back that seemed to be uncomfortable.

"Here, let me get that for you," Damien replied right on cue and she immediately handed him the bag. Steve and Sarah mumbled something about seeing if any help was needed in the kitchen and Damien followed them into the restaurant with the bag leaving me a quiet chance to meet yet another family member.

"He's very attentive," she said watching my friends as they left.

"He is great, really great!" I smiled back at her trying not to notice how often she had commented on my fiancé. She finally turned her full attention on me.

"So, like I said before, I'm really sorry I couldn't have come sooner. Bertie said you were in trouble, but I wasn't sure where you were, or I would have gotten to you first. Are they treating you well here; training you and what not?" she questioned with a tilt of her head.

"The coven have been very informative and accommodating, but they said I had to wait for Bertie to get back before I could be properly trained. They were kind of secretive about the whole thing so you can imagine my anxiety." I chuckled nervously.

"That's one of the things I will never miss about this place. There are just too many secrets here. They at least told you that I was coming, right?" She twisted her gum in her mouth like a nervous gesture which made her look younger than she was.

Deciding to be completely honest, I took a deep breath and said, "I didn't even know you existed until you just pulled up. I didn't know about Gram either until yesterday. They seem to like surprises around here." I left no amount of sarcasm out.

"Oh child, you ain't seen nothing yet," she said, shaking her head sadly. "Why don't

you update me on the situation? Bertie was pretty brief on the way over." I quickly went over the highlights starting with the scene at the motel and ending with me coming over the hill. I was careful to leave out the part about visiting my parents. I wasn't sure how she would react to me 'seeing' them although she didn't seem surprised to find out that I could see spirits of those that had passed. Everyone else seemed to have their secrets here, only fair I got to keep one.

"Geez," was all she said when I was finished. She appeared to be in deep thought, then one of the coven members came out and told us that lunch was ready. I had to learn their names soon if I planned on staying here, it was rude to just keep referring to them as old ladies and witches. "Sure, sure," she said, mindlessly waving a hand at the woman but still standing perplexed, looking at the ground in great concentration like she was trying to make it move. At this point, I didn't think it would surprise me if she did, given that we all seemed to carry some unusual gift that had brought us together. I felt guilty for unloading on her so completely, but she had stated that she disliked the antics that went on here and lying would have been one of them. We continued to stand in silence as questions and anxiety began to swirl in me. Strong hands tugged my shoulders and led me away from my aunt, who remained still as a statue in the parking lot. I recognized Damien's cologne and was grateful for the save. Had I frightened her? She didn't seem the type that would be scared easily so I shook that thought from my mind.

The comforting aromas of the eatery greeted us as we went inside, but I couldn't think about food. She seemed so eager to help me before, but now she stood outside alone, frozen in an expression that I didn't know her well enough to interpret. I wish they had told me about her before she showed up so I could have prepared a story that wouldn't have been so jaw dropping. I had so many questions of my own too that I had yet to express. Like, why were Gram and her arguing? Was there some bad blood there I needed to know about? How is it that I had no pictures of her or why, better yet, didn't she come and get me? I'm sure after the tragedy that took my parents, she could have protected me. These questions would have to wait until I had more time alone with her and I had gotten a better sense of who she was. For now, I would focus on getting through this meal and then tackling the big things.

The table seemed extra packed as Aunt Dawn (I guess I'll call her that) had finally come inside and grabbed a plate like nothing was wrong. The conversations around the tables were just as vague as they had been before, like no one seemed to notice. At least I got to hear more about the others' training from the morning while Gram and I were getting to know each other better in the woods. Steve was excited to be included in the exercises since his powers had yet to be acknowledged, and the defensive moves that Sam was teaching him were something that he fantasized about using when we got back home. We all left the word 'home' floating in the air, wondering when we would ever return and if things would ever go back to the way they were. Sarah and I didn't have any real family at home to worry about us, but I knew that if Damien and Steve didn't get back when scheduled, their mom would be on the warpath looking for them wondering why they hadn't come home to do their laundry yet. We still had time left, but it felt like it had been months since we were home last. We had started out on this trip, naive and unaware of how it would change us. Who knew how safe we would be if we left our protective circle? Would they have to come back with us for us to feel safe in our beds again?

My body ached for my bed and just the thought of sleeping in the booth again made my back hurt. I wouldn't be able to stand it here much longer, and I doubted my friends were up to more nights sleeping in a restaurant only to wake to more training and not the fun we had planned on when we had started the week. Maybe it was the stress, the constant fear, or just the desire to be normal, but I longed to feel warm sand between my toes and the hot sun on my back. I should dismiss the thought, I know, but I could still dream, couldn't I?

Lunch left me with more questions than breakfast had, but I had no time for anything but cleaning the table and awaiting my next lesson outside with everyone else. Steve and Sarah were paired up again with the martial arts defense specialist Sam, while Damien and I waited patiently for our teacher. The time we had alone together was brief, broken by my newfound aunt and a string of profanities being thrown at my grandmother. As they approached, we caught a few choice words that I didn't care to repeat but overall, she was mad at Gram for not informing her sooner about something. Apparently, what I had said didn't surprise her but enraged her, to the point that we had to keep our distance from her due to her energy bubble she had puffed out again.

"It's like standing too close to a furnace. The further we go away from her, the cooler I feel." Damien remarked. Since it was naturally hot in the South this time a year, you can't imagine the level of heat she had to be putting off to even feel it over the weather. It's a wonder our clothes didn't catch fire.

"Pretty cool, though. Wonder if I'll be that powerful someday." I thought allowed.

"Would make it harder to be around you when you're PMSing." Damien joked. I lightly punched him in the arm, but I felt closer to my aunt after seeing how much we had in common when it came to Gram's mysteries. Her waves of anger showed that she had a power that appeared to be very strong and familiar. It was like her power recognized mine and instead of burning me like it did Damien, it caressed me with warm phantom fingers. Gram and Dawn noticed us as they rounded the corner, and they went quiet. Gram threw on a quick smile while Dawn focused on a place near her foot.

"Okay kids, are you ready for another hour of lessons," she said smiling. We all

smiled back at her pretending we had not just overheard them yelling. "Good, so Steven and Sarah already left with Sam for more defense practice." We both nodded in unison and pointed to the field where the group was already getting started. I silently hoped that Dawn and I would get some alone time to get to know each other better for our training assignment. Gram took another soothing breath, "Damien, you and Marty are going to do some training in the woods this afternoon. I think I saw her heading in that direction in preparation. Go ahead now, don't dawdle." Damien looked back at me reluctantly, afraid to leave me alone with the two angry adults, but I nodded towards him as he left pouting. He was even cuter when he pouted.

"So I guess it's just me left," I said looking at Gram and Aunt Dawn for some sort of hint as to what I would be doing. Maybe there would be some actual training. I didn't have many days left to train or time to get to know more about my new family's dynamic before the battle would be here.

"Jo, you and Dawn will be training for the rest of the afternoon. I need to rest for a while anyway and she is anxious to get to know you better." She waved us off and hobbled back into the building. I looked at my aunt, trying to contain my glee on getting to do what I wanted all along.

"Well, we better get started. From what I hear, we don't have much time." I nodded in agreement as I followed her in silence behind the restaurant. She didn't seem too pleased to be training me but she hadn't appeared happy since her arrival, so

I wasn't going to take it personally. She may be incapable of expressing joy, which I deeply hoped was not a family trait.

"I'm really excited to learn whatever it is you're here to teach me, but I thought I needed some kind of object or something before I could..." she suddenly stopped and turned towards me with a sour look on her face.

.   "Out of all the ladies in the coven, I'm the only one with abilities like yours and apparently, that qualifies me to teach you. Trust me, if you hadn't told me everything and I didn't feel you were in danger, we wouldn't be here doing this at all. But here we are!" She threw her arms out on either side of her body showing her exasperation. Okay? Not a great start. "Let's make the best of it, I guess. Tell me about your last conversation with your spirit guide, I think it would help us find our starting point." Gram hadn't spilled the knowledge that my parents were my guides. Maybe she wanted me to tell Dawn but right now I didn't want to upset her further.

"I was told that a "Trickster" was coming for me because I had the ability to stop him. I don't see how *I* can when a whole coven couldn't. I know I'm not as powerful as they are." I explained.

"It's not how powerful you are, but the power you possess. You're like your mother, your power is unique." She winced when she mentioned my mother, but whatever emotion had been there, was gone just as quick. "With it, the dark entities think they can twist your power into a weapon they can use for domination."

"You think I have the ability to control souls? To trap them in what, bottles or something to be sold on the black market?" I honestly had no idea what you were supposed to gain from imprisoning ghosts. Be a ghostbuster or something?

"Your Mother did, once, and I know she could have done it again many times over.

From what the old lady tells me, you had trouble in the motel room. She said it was your first time encountering something of that nature. I believe the mistakes made there will help us figure out what areas we need to improve on." Did she not know that the motel room had been a complete wash? We didn't even get through the cleansing before I was dragged outside unconscious. Plenty of improvements could be made since nothing went right, so where to begin?

"I'm not sure if you know this but, nothing during the cleansing, or exorcism (whatever) worked. We walked in and Gram spoke a few words. The next thing I know, the room started attacking us in the form of arms coming from the walls. I passed out after that." I still hadn't told anyone about the vision I had had in detail, and I hoped I would never have to discuss it. I wanted to go back to the motel and solve its mystery, but if I were to do it, it would be on my terms.

"I had a similar experience my first time, too. The old lady said it would benefit us to see how a home cleansing is done, but I still don't think it was appropriate to take two *eight-year-olds* to such a thing. Man was I scared! Of course, she had warned us a little ahead of time what we were getting into. Your Mom went unconscious first, and then I soon followed. I'm not sure if you know this or not, but your mother and I are twins. We shared more than just good looks, we shared gifts too. What she felt in that house carried over to me. Before I passed out, I saw flashes of chaos across my eyes that included the family that had lived there before. The mother had gone crazy and while her husband was away on business. They had some kids and well, it was bad. I know because I had glimpses of it while I was unconscious. Unfortunately, Sunny got the worst of it in all its gruesome glory." My Mom's name spoken out loud sent chills across my arms causing goose bumps. Or maybe it was the story; either way I crossed my arms over my chest against the sudden chill.

"We hadn't learned how to shield yet, even from one another's emotions, but after that accident, we practiced tuning out until it became easier. The whole mess was a disaster for us, but the crazy witch was able to turn a negative into a positive by finding her spirit guide there. She had just become a novice in her craft and a guide is something that definitely brought her up to an abecedarian level for witches." Dawn shook her head and rested her hand to her temple. "Her guide turned out to be the oldest child killed who wasn't much older than we were at the time. She hadn't had a long fulfilling life, she wasn't even a teen yet, and we could feel the regret seeping from her aura. I suppose it didn't bother her, not much ever does," she sighed then collected herself to continue.

"Once we were outside the house, the witch grinned down at us with such enjoyment in her eyes, but we both felt terrible for witnessing the murder of our neighboring family. Needless to say, our relationship with our mother was also changed." I set in silence trying to mull everything over; so much new information and most of it was very similar to my own trials and tribulation with Gram. She had been throwing me into things unaware since our first meeting. I had taken from her story that for one, the old witch is crazy, and for another, instead of feeling like an outcast, I had a family full of unusual people, just like me. I could be accepted here with Dawn; I wouldn't have to be ashamed of who I was. I had to hide the enjoyment I was feeling from my Aunt who was frowning at me and probably thought my glee was a sign of a twisted sense of humor.

"So who is Gram's spirit guide?" I asked, hoping it wasn't the little girl from the college with the blood stained dress.

"A pre-teen girl named Sophie that was one of the oldest of the household."

"What did she look like?" I asked, hoping that my inquiring wasn't too suspicious.

"She was about 4 and a half feet tall, or so, with blonde hair and big eyes. I saw more of her after she passed than when she was alive. It was so weird having a ghost girl at the breakfast table in the morning, but the hag wouldn't listen to our protests of having her around. She wanted to be in constant contact in case something came across that she needed to know right away. Sometimes they would have the weirdest conversations!" She seemed to trail off in deep thought and all I could think of was how exciting this all was!

My mom was a twin, Gram was even crazier than I could have imagined, and her spirit guide was definitely the little girl I saw at school. I kind of already knew that last part, but confirmation was always good. I was glad my Aunt had similar abilities as me, it would make her my trainer and not my secretive grandmother. I knew I would have more confidence with Dawn training me and I would be able to hear the dead again in no time because of it.

After Dawn's big backstory was over, she explained more about spirit guides and how they come about. I realized that my parents weren't the guides I had thought they were since they had passed on and normally your spirit guide is one that is stuck on our plane. Instead, they must be guardians since they had no 'real' reach on this plane of existence. I needed to find my guide, or travel guide as I so lovingly nicknamed it in my head, to achieve the next level. I was anxious to find out who it was going to be, but there were plenty of other things for me to learn in the meantime. I chose not to share this with Dawn, as I felt it would only hold things up further.

Training went long after the sun went down, and we were all exhausted when we met up in the diner. Supper was light since it was late but the conversations were livelier then we felt. Sarah had learned some new moves plus she was getting better at meditating. During her trances, she had been able to project her power further into the woods where she could feel the presence of every insect or animal for yards. Her goal was to be able to reach town which had to be ten miles or more away from the coven.

Steve was excited that he was learning how to attack in 'stealth mode'. He kept sneaking up behind the older women and tapping them on random shoulders. By the time they had turned around, he had already returned to his seat with his fork halfway to his mouth. Sarah called him her little Ninja. Damien spoke of his training with Marty, and he boasted how powerful she was.

"I'm telling you, she blasted this tree, but you couldn't see any damage to it; then WHAM!!!! It just fell over! When it was on the ground, I went over to check it out and I saw it was completely hollow. It was like she totally hollowed it out!" He was so amazed and his smile reflected his enthusiasm for his new trade. I could visualize the madness when we got back home and he tried to work his magic on the shrubbery in his parent's yard.

"I think Sam could still kick Marty's butt if it came down to a real fight! Hell, I would pay to see that!" Steve replied in between bits of dinner. I tried to stay out of the path of his projectile food as I mulled over everything I had learned. I might not have learned how to blast a tree hollow or how to sneak attack my enemies, but what I had learned made me feel more confident about our new team taking out our adversaries. I felt, for the first time, like we all might have a chance to survive against the darkness. It turned out that my new family was strong and nowhere near as weak as I had originally understood. I had a desire to see how we would measure up against the coming war.

Chapter Eighteen
REALITY CHECK

THE end of the week came up suddenly and conversations about what we planned to do about school were scattered. We knew we weren't done here but school would start in the next few days and some of us were more scared about that then the upcoming battle. By some of us, I mean Sarah.

"It's not that I mind putting school off until after we save the world, it's just that I'll be disappointing my teachers when I don't return in time. Not to mention losing my financial aid." Sarah pouted. She truly cared more about what the teachers thought then the education she'd miss. At this point, I didn't see the future classes as a loss since there may not be a school left for me to go back to, or a job for me to join if I lost this fight. I was still foggy on what this big bad evil planned to do, but I knew that if we didn't defeat him, the world would be his playground of chaos.

"Hun, just think how proud they will be when they hear how you saved the planet! We'll be seeing As across the board for all of us!" Steve smiled his big cheesy grin as we folded our bedsheets. I liked Steve's optimism, but I feared life would never be that simple for me again, even if we won. Who would we want to return to their normal (okay, normal for me) life after everything we had seen? Plus, I had blood relatives now! Something that was still new to me, but I wanted to learn more. There was just too much to process for me to give school a second thought.

"Your grades will finally be passing! I was getting so tired of Dad's old jokes about putting you in Clown School or Ronald McDonald College." Damien playfully poked his brother who poked him back in response and soon, they were rolling around the floor, being 'boys'. This conversation wasn't getting them any closer to a decision, but it was a nice way to avoid the inevitable. I knew *I* had to stay. College would be there later for me perhaps, but Sarah needed school. She needed the challenging courses, the strict teachers, and oh my God, the studying because that was who she was. It had been her dream since she finally got away from her uncle and came to live with me in the foster home. She wanted to be a schoolteacher so she could repay the teacher that took an interest in her and made the call to CPS that changed her life. Without Sarah, the world would be deprived of an educator that would really care about her students. I had to make sure she got back; she deserved that life.

"I think what Damien meant was...we're going to stay here and fight! No way could I go back now!" Steve yelled out of breath as Damien pinned him on the floor. They both had big sly grins on their faces. It would be nice if at least the guys stayed with me. They'd probably have no regrets, either. Sarah remained pouting at them while my mind continued to swirl around thoughts of our future. One thing I kept falling back on was the idea of anyone getting hurt. I would never recover from that loss. I still wanted to get my friends far away from all of this, but I knew Damien wouldn't leave me behind and his brother wouldn't let him stay back without him. That just left Sarah.

"Sarah, you should go back." I said in all seriousness, staring out into space, afraid to meet her eyes. "You've dreamt about being a teacher since we were small and you're so close to getting your degree. I don't want my drama to get in the way of that." With her ability she also could 'feel' if something went wrong. Then she could run and hide far away from it. It was a win-win in my book. Either scenario, she would be happy and safe.

"I couldn't bear the thought of leaving you all and running." Sarah came over to me and lightly placed her hand on my shoulder. "I appreciate that you think you're giving me a choice but I'm not going anywhere. You're stuck with me." She chuckled and it made me smile despite my feelings. She took a seat next to me on the booth. "I guess it just felt better to talk about *normal* things for once instead of magic and mysterious truckers." She glanced around the room as if searching for approval from all of us. Steve got off the floor and reached for Sarah's hand as he squeezed into the booth next to her.

"It's settled then," Damien said dusting off his jeans, "we're all staying and seeing this through." He placed his arm around me and gave my shoulder a squeeze. Sarah jumped as if struck by lightning.

"What are you going to do about the apartment and your folks?"

"Dad is going on a business trip and Mom is going to spend some time with her sister in Covington for a few weeks. I called them yesterday and checked in. They won't notice we're gone for a while. We'll think of something to tell them when the time comes," Damien replied as I scooted over to allow him more space in the booth next to me.

"Our place is paid up till the end of the month. That will give us a couple of weeks before the landlord gets worried. As long as we keep our weekly calls to Momma D and drop into town for more supplies; we should be good." I was already making a mental note to get more deodorant for the guys as I discreetly moved Damien's arm from around my shoulder.

"Should we call the school then? At least tell them we're not coming back this semester?" Sarah asked still looking a tad sad when she mentioned school. Most dropouts didn't inform the schools about their intentions on not returning. Only Sarah would worry about such a silly thing. I still nodded at her sympathetically instead of cracking the smile I could feel coming on.

"We could tell them the truth; call them up and say, 'We won't be able to finish this semester due to impending doom only we can stop.' Oh don't worry, we'll be careful!" Sarah frowned at Steve making fun of her question. We all started laughing heartily which grabbed the attention of some of the witches busying themselves in the restaurant. They gave us funny looks but never stopped to ask what was so funny. Gram and Dawn weren't among them, and I pictured them outside raising a fuss (along with a crowd) about the day's progress. Secretly, Dawn had told me she didn't believe we'd be safe here forever. Her philosophy had been 'it's harder to hit a rolling stone' and I had to agree. Even with the protective spell and the odd witches sitting outside the building, I didn't feel completely guarded at night. If anything, I felt watched.

I didn't see fit to share my paranoia with the group, so I had kept it to myself, but my suspicions were getting stronger. What if they were waiting, just outside our barriers, looking for a weakness so they could attack us? Just thinking these thoughts made me feel claustrophobic in the eatery and I excused myself to go outside for air. I wanted to be alone for a moment to think clearly about our time spent here so far and if we would be prepared for an impending attack.

I needed to speak to Dawn but looking out into the dark, all I could see was phantom shapes of tents and shadows moving around the torches placed throughout the yard. Snores were mixed with murmurs as some of the ladies were building up the fire in the middle. I imagined I was looking at a refugee camp, with people tossed about here and there, chanting or dancing around the flames. I felt envious of their courage to sleep exposed amongst the night while we slept inside a brick building. At least if a fight came, we had shelter, but they felt protected behind their magical field. I wanted to feel that security too but all I kept thinking was *'they* will find us, and *they're* plotting our demise. You know, all the fun stuff. Granted, the training we'd been receiving for the last few days had made some of us feel more confident about the outcome of the upcoming confrontation, but it didn't make me feel any better. Training and sleeping in a clearing surrounded by trees and darkness; how could I find comfort in that?

The door opened behind me, and Damien's arms encircled my waist. He remained quiet, allowing me to take comfort in his embrace instead of feeling pressured to express my thoughts. Even though we trained separately and spent most of our time apart, I felt closer to him. Maybe it was the impending peril or the fact that he had really grown in the last week, who knew? I was so fortunate to find a man who could accept me so completely even after he had met the family I didn't know I had. My Gram is a living testament that the ladies in my gene pool turn senile in their older age and my aunt's rage showed how out of control our power can be. My lack of crazy now was a true testament of my devotion to him, even though my family genes were making me question how much more I could handle.

He nuzzled my neck, and I could feel the beard bristles against my skin. Another mental note, get more razors in town. I leaned back into him, taking in the smell of his skin mixed with the musky scent of the woods where he had been practicing with Marty. Marty's skills as a teacher had astounded me but I had found many of the witches' talents to be a surprise. There were two twins that were in their late thirties, who could feel or see glimpses of the underworld. I guess you could say one could 'see' and the other could 'feel' but they both creeped me out. They were a good warning system if the damned souls there were on the move against us, but mostly they just gossiped about what celebrities were in Hell.

The Buck Sisters (Buck was the short version of their last name) came to the group back when my Gram was finishing high school. The oldest one, Susie, was a grade or two further than Gram but the younger sister Ember, was in the same grade. Apparently, the Buck Sisters had a lot of trouble with their abilities and even burnt down a trailer or a whole park of them (the story got bigger every time one of them told it). Together, they had the ability to cause explosions but apart, they could only start small fires. They came in handy when the burner went out on the stove but sometimes their aim wasn't spot on. We always kept a fire extinguisher near them, needless to say.

Some of the other ladies hadn't revealed anything extraordinary but they knew how to work the spells and brew the potions. Steve called them the 'Potion Masters' and they primarily stayed together with their heads down, no doubt trying to come up with a new spell or brew of some kind. The oldest of the group was rumored to be in her eighties but I'm not sure if there was any truth to that. She had hung up her robe years ago but didn't feel right retiring altogether, so she stuck around and provided support to the masses. I noticed a lot of the ladies referred to her as Mom. Other women had been with her long enough to feel that comfortable, but Gladys worked for me just fine.

"How are you holding up?" Damien whispered to me.

"Pretty well I guess. I'm still not used to all of this just yet or my new family members. I guess sometimes you just need to get a little air, or you feel like you're suffocating." I forced a smile up at him.

"This whole trip has been a lot for you to take in, I know, but you're a strong woman and I have confidence that you'll be able to make heads or tails of all of this soon enough. Everything happens for a reason."

"You're starting to sound like Gram. It just seems like this whole thing has been dumped on me all at once. I just don't know anything about what we're going up against besides the fact that he feels threatened by me, which I find hard to believe."

"Maybe you would feel better if we went to the library in town and looked him up. I overheard some coven members say that there's been documentation of him before and we could check it out while we're getting supplies," Damien suggested.

"That's a really great idea, Damien! I knew I loved you for more than your dashing good looks." I nuzzled his shoulder and smiled up at him. A thought crossed my mind, and the smile began to fade.

"What's wrong?" he asked.

"Gram doesn't want anyone to go to town for fear that he might have minions there that will follow us back here. She'll never let us go. It would've been nice to get out of here, though." I laid my head on his shoulder and continued looking up at the sky.

"I'm sure when we convince her that you must know your enemy inside and out to be a good fighter, she'll let us have a little time at the library. Training isn't the only thing that can prepare us when we know diddly about this evil guy. Besides, I'm sure they need supplies too and I'll go with you for protection." He puffed out his chest and made himself appear taller.

"You know that trick only works on bears, right?" I stated jokingly.

"Hey, it still makes me look intimidating, anyway. It's getting chilly, how about we head back in, and we can start on the old lady tomorrow?" I nodded my head in agreement and went back into the building with him hand in hand. It was going to be hard to convince her that we needed to go but she couldn't stop me if I didn't want to stay. I had been compliant up to this point, but I could certainly be defiant if I wanted to. I hoped that side of me wouldn't have to come out, but I was going stir crazy here, and I needed to get out and see other people as confirmation that they did exist.

Sleeping was tough but I devised a plan to talk her into letting us go. Steve and Sarah agreed to stay so she wouldn't feel like she was giving in so completely and their staying behind was a good faith sign that I would be back. No way would I leave them behind normally, but we couldn't see any way around it and they were happy to oblige. In the morning we put our plan into action after breakfast was cleared away. I saw the old broad sitting outside smoking what appeared to be a long pipe with what I hoped was tobacco.

"Gram's I...." she cut me off.

"Yes, yes I know what you're here to ask but before I say yes, may I remind you to be careful around the locals, they don't take kindly to us 'tree-huggers'. I can't imagine why they think we're hippies just because we practice in nature. Close-minded 'normies' are what they are." She took another puff and stared out across the field in deep thought. "Good luck finding anything in that library of theirs useful. Last time I was in there, all they had was some Judy Bloom novels and a monitor that ran microfilm. Better hope they got internet out here in the boonies." She blew out a cloud of smoke and shifted in her seat, still favoring her injured leg. I stood there shocked and unable to respond. I had come expecting a fight or at least an argument but here she was completely compliant to demands I hadn't even made. How did she know what I was going to ask?

"Well, don't stand there all whopper-jawed. What did you think? I couldn't be reasonable?" She seemed more irritable then usual today. "Besides, this way it keeps us from fighting or you sneaking off. I plan on sending some of the gals out with you so you won't be going alone." She turned to finally look at me. "I suppose Damien will go too but the girls need supplies, and they know the right shops to get them from. Currency around here is a bit tight, but we trade things where we can." She glanced up at the position of the sun and shielded her eyes with a wrinkled hand. "You better get going, I told them to be ready after breakfast." She motioned with her arm in the direction of the van, and I noticed some of the witches loading boxes into it. She was still transfixed on the horizon in front of her, but I nodded anyway, unable to talk, and headed towards the parked van. Damien came out and met me while I was heading away from the building.

"So, how'd it go?" he asked anxiously.

"Just give me a minute, I'm still trying to wrap my head around what just happened." My steps became slower as I thought it over. "It was like she knew what I was going to ask her before the words ever left my mouth. How did she know?" I asked aloud.

"What's it matter, right? Did she say yes?" Damien; always direct and to the point.

"Yeah, the witches over by the van are going to take us to the library while they shop. We've got a couple of hours to research I'm sure, while they do their trading." I was speaking in a monotone, still too shocked to express any feeling while rolling Gram's one-sided conversation over in my head. Damien took note of my tone and just walked silently next to me. Had one of my friends went to her first and told her what we were up to? No, I knew their loyalty stood with me. Did she have some of the witches eavesdropping on us? That seemed more realistic but there hadn't been one in the restaurant last night when we concocted our plan. I was pretty sure none of the ladies had any psychic powers or I would have asked them by now how the upcoming battle was going to go. Maybe when I got back, I could ask her directly but for now, I needn't look a gift-horse in the mouth.

I recognized some of the ladies when I approached, and I knew why they were chosen for this mission. Bertie was there I guess in case we snuck off and she needed to track us, Lillie (dressed as a lumberjack again) because of her complete loyalty to Marge, and Crystal, the skinny dark-haired lady that I had tried to squeeze information out of the first night we were here. I couldn't imagine what her purpose in coming was, she was one of the younger members of the group and maybe she just wanted to get out of here like us. There were a few others I didn't have names for yet, but I was sure there was a logical reason they were chosen to join. We all nodded to one another, but no one spoke as we climbed into the back of the old van.

The interior looked like you would expect from the outside, split upholstery and a bare floor where carpet had once been. The inside windows were covered in a thin layer of brown dust and they didn't appear to open at all explaining the stale odor that hit you when you got in. The van was probably one of the reasons the town folk thought they were hippies. It certainly looked like it belonged to some before the coven had come across it. I guess that would be a question for another time. Damien was having a hard time adjusting the seatbelt over his bulky frame and I found that mine wouldn't pull out far enough to clasp with the lower belt. So much for protecting me; what if one of these geriatrics feel asleep behind the wheel and we crashed?

"I'll hang on to you," Damien said after he too gave up on his belt and he put his arm around me. I know it wasn't the safest way to travel but we did what we had to, and I knew the ladies would be careful or they would have Gram to report to.

The witches piled in after us along with some crates they had brought along with them that contained jars filled with some kind of grayish liquid. I guessed that was what they planned on trading with, but I couldn't imagine what they were or who would pay for them. I was thankful the jars contained lids that trapped the smell that I was sure was just begging to escape and invade our nostrils. What a lovely trip this would be!

Chapter Nineteen

TOO MUCH SOUTHERN HOSPITALITY CAN LEAD TO HOSTILITY

THE trip was a quiet and surprisingly quick one to town. When we stopped and got out, I took a look around for any landmarks that could give me a better idea of where we were but the only thing that was visible was an old gas station and a strip mall. The station looked as dirty as the inside of the van was and appeared to only have one working pump. Its sign hung from one chain while the other end hung loosely, revealing rust. I would guess it had seen this town when it was only a dirt road, and the population was below 100. The strip mall wasn't in great shape but it appeared to be the only prominent fixture left that time had been kind to. Many of the spaces available were empty with signs stating they were for lease. A Discount Tobacco stood on one end and an old RC Cola vending machine marked its entrance. Various signs hung in the window displaying different varieties of products on sale and an older gentleman dressed in farmer's clothing hung outside the door as he finished his last drag.

I wondered where the ladies planned on doing their trading and then I noticed the Bait and Tackle shop on the other end. It seemed to be the hot spot in town as a challenging game of chess was being watched by a group of men outside. It seemed the masters of the board were two older folks, one woman wearing overalls and a straw hat and a fella sporting a sunburned head. We could tell they were closing on the end of their game due to the lack of pieces left on the table. Hoots and shouts of encouragement were coming from the surrounding men. The witches started towards the tackle shop which read 'The Bass Pole' and the humor wasn't lost on us as we approached. Some of the coven members shifted uncomfortably while holding their containers of merchandise. The others spread out like they were looking for something, or someone. I didn't bother to ask, I was just enjoying being out in the 'real' world again.

"Ya all go on in, I'll be done with this old coot in a minute," said the lady with the straw hat never taking her eyes off the board. The men that overshadowed the table stepped back to allow us a wide enough berth to enter. None of them bothered to make eye contact and some looked as though they were transfixed on something interesting on the ground. Once inside the shop, we were amazed to see the variety that she offered there. Row after row of items were sprawled before us and stand-up fridges along one wall were full of different sized Styrofoam bowls. A poster of a worm on a hook read, "Got Fish?" and below it stood a smaller fridge with cold cans of cola inside.

"I'll grab us some cokes before we walk over to the library." Damien strolled over to the fridge while I waited for the cashier to come back to the counter from wherever they were hiding.

"We'll cover that for ya. It will probably be a while until she's done, anyway. The library is down the side road a piece next to the Post Office. Shouldn't miss it," said Bertie as she and the other gals looked for a place to lay their boxes full of goo jars.

"Thanks," I said as Damien came back with two frosty cans in his hand. "We shouldn't be long."

"We know where you'll be," said Lillie not looking up as she made a twirling motion in the air. I knew I should have found that comforting but for some reason, I didn't. Damien opened the door for me as we proceeded to walk to the book sanctuary. The chess game seemed to be getting more heated as we wedged out the door into the bright light outside. We had very little time before we had to be back to the coven, and I wanted to get as much done as I could so there was no time to waste watching the event unfold.

"So do you think we'll be able to find what we need?" Damien asked as he opened his can to take a sip.

"I hope they at least have the internet but who knows way out here?" I opened my can as well and took a big gulp, letting the carbonation tickle my nose. We took the narrow road that looked to lead to a building that read Post office on the side as we tried to finish our drinks. The town appeared to be deserted besides the commotion in front of the bait shop and the random witches standing about, but the scenery was still surreal. Tall trees towered over us, shading our path as the late flowers of the spring swayed in the slight breeze. I smelled lilac and the familiar scent of honeysuckle being carried on the wind and down the path as we took in the silence around us. It was nice to just listen to nature for once since living with multiple women meant constant chatter.

"Hey, this is the first time we have been alone all week," I admitted out loud, gripping his hand.

"Yeah, it's nice," he agreed as he placed an arm across my shoulders and pulled me in towards his side. "Makes you almost forget about the danger we're in." He smiled down at me with worry still in his eyes. I knew the question I wanted to ask would ruin the moment, but it had been bothering me and I didn't know when I would get another chance to ask.

"So, how long did you have to keep your powers a secret from me?" He choked on his coke. "I'm not mad or anything that you didn't tell me right away, I get that. I just wanted to use this rare opportunity to talk about being honest with each other. I saw you with the guy at the hotel, you know, before Gram got there." He stopped and regarded me for a moment before he answered.

"I haven't known long. I was going to tell you, really, but I wasn't sure what was going on myself. I kind of got into this disagreement with a guy at school before we left, and when I went to shove him, well, he sort of flew back into the lockers harder than I meant to shove him. There was this burst of light and then he was slumped on the floor and the locker had a new dent in it." My face had to have shown my surprise because he hesitated before continuing. "Don't worry he's fine...but I saw this dark light flare up between us when I hit him. I thought maybe I was just seeing things, so I shrugged it off until I did it again with that creepo spirit back at the hotel. I still wasn't sure how it had happened till your grandma showed up spouting that stuff about us both coming together for a purpose, because of our abilities. It just clicked for me then. I wanted to tell you but I knew you would get that worried look on your face, like you do now, and I didn't want to ruin our trip." He gently stroked my arm. "I'm sorry, from here on out, I won't wait to tell you if I do something weird, okay?" He smiled his genuine smile at me and I eased back under his arm again with a small hug. It must have been so scary for him, not knowing what had happened or if it would happen again. I could relate.

"They didn't suspend you, or anything? For the fight I mean?"

"No, the guy said he tripped when I shoved him. I don't think he saw the same light or if he did, he didn't say anything about. I was scared at first but now, I'm just glad I get to help protect you in a way I wouldn't have been able to before." He kissed the side of my head, and I looked up at him with a smile. It's true, having Damien at my side through all of this was my only real comfort, but I still wished that he and our friends could run instead of feeling like they needed to protect me.

"Is that it?" Damien asked pointing to a building but unconvinced that we had almost arrived. This old place could be full of history and have books dating back to the town's beginning but the outside looked discouraging. Just because it was in desperate need of paint, and some of its shingles were missing didn't mean it wouldn't hold what we had come for. A red wagon sat outside the building overflowing with children's book such as, "If you Give a Mouse a Cookie" and "Everyone Poos", with a sign hanging from it advertising the books for sale at a quarter a piece. There were a few children scurrying around it, anxiously awaiting their turn to dive through the stack and find a treasure there that was waiting for them to open it. Damien and I walked past them, up the stone steps to the big brown double doors that stood closed in front of us. Our conversation would have to wait till this part was over.

Once inside, it took my eyes a few minutes to adjust to the dimness. A couple of tables were scattered about on my right and a lone desk stood to my left with a computer on it. I took that to be a good sign as we both continued further within the book depository. In the very back, great shelves stood to the ceiling covered in colorful paper and hardbacks. Little white chairs set before them, decorated in flowers and bright red fruits. I assumed this was the kiddy section and it would be one less place for us to wander in search of the information we'd come for. More shelves further down stood spaced apart to my right and they were labeled as Fiction and Non-fiction. If we had to resort to books, I had no idea if Fiction or Non-fiction would be what we needed. As of last week, if you would have asked me about the 'Trickster' or his minions, I would have told you it sounded like Fiction and not very good fiction at that.

Nope, a computer with internet would have to do, and luckily, we had seen at least that addition back at the entrance. A door stood closed past what looked to be the Librarian's desk, and it had a set of familiar rules listed on it, most of them referring to the usage of computers and the lack of food or drink past this point. Damien and I had disposed of our cans outside, knowing that drinks would most likely be banned, and we were very knowledgeable in the usage of computers, so we glanced over the list for anything additional that we needed to know. Unfortunately, according to the list, you needed a code to access the internet which could only be obtained by the librarian. The small window at the top of the locked door showed that the room was dark, and it appeared there was no one in it. I tried the handle just in case and, sure enough, locked. I hoped that we hadn't come all this way just to be stopped by a locked door.

"We just need to find the librarian," I said as I glanced around for any sign of life in the place. The building seemed deserted besides us and the kids outside so, my first thought was to ask the kids. They must know where the librarian is or at least when they would be back. I left Damien to search the inside while I retreated out to find a kid and ask them where everyone was.

The first one I came to looked to be about five or six but eager to help a grown-up, even though I was a stranger. He had on overalls that were stained from playing in the dirt and a striped shirt that still had some ice cream clinging to it. He pointed to the side of the building as an answer to my question and I noticed puffs of smoke coming from beyond it. I thanked the kid and jogged over to the side of the building where I found a rather young looking girl puffing away on a device.

"Are you the librarian here?" I asked the girl.

"Yeah, just started my break, do ya mind?" I shook my head. So much for southern hospitality.

"I just need the computer if that's possible." I said trying to give her a genuine smile but knowing that it failed around the edges.

"Sure, ya got a card, right?" she asked blowing smoke in my face. Lovely. She knew I was a stranger that wouldn't have a card but I continued smiling at her anyway.

"No actually, would my card from back home help?" I tried for a friendly tone, but my anger was coming through. I took my bag from my shoulder and reached in for my wallet as Damien was coming around the corner.

"Hey, Jo, I thought you might need a hand, you were taking a while." He smiled over at us and I could see the girl's face change. She seemed like she would be a lot more corporative with him than she had been with me so I gestured at him, hoping he would get the hint to come on over. Her eyes followed his movements as he walked towards us. I managed to clear my throat loudly to get her attention back on me.

"This is my friend Damien, he wanted to use the internet, so I came out here and found you." Damien gave me a weird look when I introduced him as my friend, but I nodded and smiled at the girl. A look came over his face and I could tell he recognized what I was trying to do. He smiled his award-winning smile down at the young thing and she just melted into a puddle. She put her vape in her pocket and pushed past me to Damien where she looped her arm through his and proceeded to lead him back to the library.

"I'm sure I can help you out, Damien is it? I see you're from out of town so it would just be silly of me to ask if you have a card," she giggled at her own joke. "How about a driver's license?" She smiled up at him so sweetly I thought about back handing her, but I was able to compose myself and walk silently behind them instead. Another point for me.

"Sure, I'll have to get it out of my wallet but I'm..." I let them drift off out of earshot as I hung back. I didn't want to distract Damien's performance and I felt a little jealous seeing him flirt with the cute girl. I would let them have some time to discuss her conditions of letting us on their equipment before I went back into the building. I needed time to cool off anyway. Images of me smacking the smug look off the librarian's face still floated around in my mind. Besides, it was a beautiful day to be outdoors, and I didn't mind having a moment to myself; something I rarely got back at the coven.

I walked out of the little alley and slowly retraced my steps to the entrance. Long shadows from the trees surrounding the building met me with outstretched arms like a welcoming cool embrace. The children were still playing around the wagon that held the discounted books as an older blonde girl watched over them from the side lines. Her back was turned to me, but her straight shoulders told me that she had some authority here and took her responsibilities seriously. It was nice seeing kids being so well behaved, something I rarely saw during my days in foster homes. From my position under the shade from the trees, I found peace and tranquility that a small town can offer. A few more minutes went by, and I thought it might be safe to check on Damien's progress.

As I climbed up the stairs, something in the air, thick and familiar, made me turn around. I looked to find the source but only the children and the surrounding landscape loomed in front of the building. Had I missed something before? I had been in my own head on my way back and completely overlooked something important. The area around the tall blonde girl shimmered as she proceeded to still watch over the other children. I walked back down a few more steps towards her. She heard me approach from behind her and she turned with superhuman speed that couldn't be from this plane.

I stared at the dead girl, surprised that my ability had improved enough that I could sense her presence before noticing her as one of the dead. Her sad look said that she longed to play with the children, but knew she had to keep her distance. I motioned for her to follow me up the stairs where I could speak to her without scaring the kids that were now looking up at me with confusion. She gave one last glance at a small boy with blonde hair that looked to be of some relation to her before she trailed behind me. At the top of the stairs, I made sure to check that the kiddies were once again paying attention to the books rather than us, and I turned to address the girl.

"What are you doing here?" I asked her, taking in her dark freckles in contrast to her light-colored hair.

"I wanted to watch," she said innocently. I knew she was talking about the little ones playing at the bottom of the stairs but deep down I wondered if she hadn't come to watch me. I felt paranoid but do you blame me? I silently scolded myself for not paying better attention.

"You can't be here, honey. Your time has passed on this earth, and you must go on to the next plane." I used words I thought Gram might say to sound more professional. I still had no clue as to what I was doing.

"Do I have to?" she asked giving me a pout and big puppy dog eyes. Oh jeez, this was going to be tough. What do I do if they say no?

"Sweetie, where you are going next pales in comparison to this world. There will be other children that can play *with* you, and you can go anywhere you can imagine." I bent down for her and had my hands on my knees. "Doesn't that sound like more fun than staying here?"

"I guess, but who's going to watch Gabriel while I'm gone?"

"Who is that?" I asked.

"My little brother over there; he needs me to watch over him." She pointed towards the little boy that had similar features to her.

"I'm sure your parents will do that for you. There's no need to let something like that keep you here. There's family waiting for you who need you on the other side." I didn't know this for sure, but I guessed the child had a grandparent or a great aunt or someone that had died and would be waiting for her in the light. I noticed that she wasn't really paying attention to me, her gaze was still towards the kids that were now perched on the grass with their new treasures in their laps. I felt a connection with this child, longing to be with other kids, doing something as easy as playing tag or reading a new fantasy novel under an old tree. I didn't have time for this right now and a thought crossed my mind that maybe I should just leave her be. She wasn't going anywhere (not really anyway) and I had much bigger fish to fry.

"Look, I need to go inside now, but I want you to remember what I said about going on to the light, okay? I'll be right back if you need to talk." She half-heartedly nodded at me, but I still felt a sting of regret. I should have stayed with her, but I had a small window of opportunity to work in and if I wanted to save the world, I would have to let one little ghost girl go unsaved. I had been doing it for years without any regard for the consequences, so why did I feel so terrible this time?

The weight of the door closing behind me felt like the clang of prison bars and I knew

deep down that she wouldn't be there when I got back. It took a few moments for my eyes to adjust to the dim lighting inside the building, but I saw Damien right away. The young librarian was still hanging on his every word from behind her desk. She appeared to be going through some keys that I could only assume unlocked our access to the computer with the internet. She was doing one of those loud throaty laughs at something clever he said, along with the signature hair flip that flirty girls do in the presence of attractive men.

I tried to approach quietly and unnoticed as she handed him a slip of paper with the code that could hold the key to our victory over our enemies. I was anxious to see what we could find on this 'trickster' that could tell us how to destroy him. I knew only what little Gram had told us which entailed that he would be hard (if not impossible) to kill, not to mention that he had been the cause of my parent's death. Gram said she wasn't surprised, a witch with my mother's kind of power was bound to get targeted at some time or another, but she had insisted on going her 'own way'. She still lived under the misconception that had my mother stayed in the coven with me, they could have protected us. Gladys told me later that everything happened for a reason and had we been here, the coven, my parents, me; would have died. There was a reason the ladies respected Gladys so much and part of it was due to her unfiltered honesty and wisdom, even though she no longer had enough juice to even complete a protection bubble.

The flirty librarian and my fiancé had their backs to me as I took a deep breath of the dusty confined space and took a seat in the red plastic chair that faced the computer. I located the power switch and the ancient modem roared to life like the dinosaur it was. I expected dial-up at best and I wasn't disappointed. Damien slipped me the piece of paper with the code to unlock the browser while he continued distracting the young lady. At least they had the internet, which is more than I had originally hoped for. I quickly typed in the one word I knew I had to start with: Trickster. More than 100 results and images popped up. This could take a lot longer than I had time for.

For a long time now, I had gotten the feeling that an invisible hand had been guiding me, so I hoped now to put that feeling to the test. I clicked page seven of the search results and found a word that struck me when the others did not, Loki, Norse Gods. Being the Egyptian specialist that I am, I knew the term but not the details of the religion. How did I know that this was the right site or not? Really, Loki? Was I just fishing at this point? Our time here held true value that the old witches would cash in on if we were not ready when they came to retrieve us. I put Loki in the search at the top of the page and it took me to a site where I could see the name mentioned numerous times. Listed by his name on the top of the page were the words, 'most unpredictable and certainly the most dangerous god in the Nordic pantheon'. Lest to say, my heart sank. Was this our guy?

I knew he would be a difficult task to accomplish, but to think that he was an ancient trickster from a long dead religion seemed like something from the Twilight Zone. How could a character from an ancient belief take form and walk among us in the twenty-first century? What kind of magic was this? In addition to being a magician, Loki was also a shape-shifter which explained how he was able to be seen in the form of an ordinary man that was employed as a truck driver. Why, when you have all the power in the world, would you choose to take the façade of a trucker? I had to read on. He had taken the form of a woman and had given birth to multiple children. Yuck! I was confused at the passage about Loki being a giant. He seemed to be regular sized to me. I came across another interesting fact; a chain of events caused by the trickster led to the destruction of the gods. Because of his involvement in the death of the god of goodness and perfection, Ragnarok, the end of all things falls on the world in the form of a winter that lasts for three years. Not only was this supposed 'giant' dangerous for us, but he also brought the destruction of the world before? I didn't think reading any further could depress me more but I was wrong, so wrong. This couldn't be the evil that was after me. There had to be some mistake. Finding my search to be hopeless, I looked up from the screen to see if I could get Damien's attention. The young librarian had him cornered between a short bookshelf and a metal filing cabinet, but he caught my signal and was slowly easing himself out towards the door. She of course was too clueless to understand he was trying to escape her perfectly manicured clutches, so she followed him. This provided me the opportunity to slip out and mingle amongst the tall bookshelves unseen. I was pretty sure I was being the sneakiest super-agent ever but it was short lived when Damien hollered over to me.

"Hey, Jo, she said there's a store down the street that has vape juices, buy one get one half off! We better scoot." I had no clue what he was talking about, but I figured it could be code for something, and the main thing was he wanted to go as soon as possible.

"I think I might have seen it on our drive in." I responded joining them. I had the information I came for I guessed, I only wished I had more time, but we had to go.

"I can make sure you find it," the young lady said, trying to get every last moment she could with my fiancé, ignoring me completely. I couldn't get mad at her, I had used Damien as bait, and I knew he could be very convincing when he needed to be. I was hoping, for her sake, that he would let her down easy.

"You've been really helpful already. I wouldn't feel right taking up any more of your time." She started pouting. "Now that I have a library card, I'm sure I'll be by again while we're in town." He gave her a quick pat on the shoulder, but it wasn't enough for her, and she stepped in for a hug. When she pulled back, she was blushing, and she appeared to be embarrassed.

"We're big huggers around here," she replied, trying to cover her tracks. He didn't say anything, but smiled and nodded at her, which seemed to make her feel better. Luckily, she noticed me coming up from behind them and backed off. She didn't want to be further embarrassed in front of me, no doubt. I smiled at her as I passed but I could tell I wouldn't be getting one in return. Happy to be away from the awkward moment, we both left via the big front doors without being followed. The sun shone brightly on us as we exited, and we had to cover our eyes until they adjusted. The air was stagnant and full of energy that danced along our skin and made the hairs on our arms stand up like static from a balloon.

"Jo, do you feel that?" Damien was examining his arms in front of him.

"Yeah, what is it?" Before I could ask any more questions, the ghost child appeared in front of me in a gust of wind with her hair trailing out behind her giving her the appearance of a banshee about to strike an unsuspecting victim. Karma can be a bitch.

Chapter Twenty
SURPRISE! (NOT SURPRISED)

"I wanted to watch," she repeated as she pointed her hands towards the sky like she would bring down a storm upon us right there, on the steps of the library. I looked around and was grateful to see that the children had all retreated to their homes and we were alone with the apparent vengeful spirit. She began twirling her hands that were still pointing upwards clockwise when the sidewalk started breaking up in long ribbons that stretched like long boney hands towards the stairs.

"Jo, I think we better get out of here!" Damien yelled over the sound of concrete ripping itself apart. It was a lot louder than you would think. I had forgotten that I was the only one that could see the dead girl. She could have made herself known to him, but that would have exerted more of her energy and apparently, she needed all she could get to conjure up whatever was beneath the pavement.

"There's a ghost girl here and I don't think she's going to just let us go!" I yelled over the noise while I pointed in the direction she was floating in. He shook his head like he understood, then he withdrew his medallion from his pocket. My emotions for the girl did a complete three-sixty. Instead of feeling sorry for not helping her, I now felt ignorant for not noticing her ill intentions. She had me going, though, and I wouldn't leave here with egg on my face.

"Boys and their jewelry," she said in a strange voice as she shot a gust of air at Damien, knocking the medallion from his hand where it then lodged itself into one of the new cracks in the sidewalk. He dashed down the stairs towards the shiny coin before it was consumed in the growing crater that was now emitting steam into the sky. It appears Hell itself has come to claim us! We gripped the railing of the stairs to remain on our feet and stood in shock as hands emerged from the rubble.

"Don't worry, I'm just the preshow. My husband should be along soon for the main event!" She laughed loud and throaty in a way that made her appear older than her body suggested. I wouldn't have thought a girl her age would have a husband but then it dawned on me that she must have been talking about Loki; our Trickster archenemy. It's not like I had a huge list of bad guys that wanted me dead, and he was the most likely choice. The hands grew arms that slowly emerged from the crevices. Some of the creatures attached to them had fully escaped from the steaming fire pit and I didn't know what to make of them. They were made of pieces and parts of the human skeleton. Some were missing a leg bone while others were missing rib cages. They looked like a human junkyard fused together to form a macabre army. They varied in size, but I knew better then laugh at them as they tried to function their odd moving parts. These were the creatures that Gram had warned me about days earlier, the same monsters that had stolen the souls of her friends and were now here to steal ours.

"Don't let them touch you, Damien!" I yelled, desperation in my voice. I wasn't sure if I was ready for this, but I knew I could at least warn him before it was too late. He stepped back from one of the minions that had crawled from its hiding place and was advancing on him with the surprising speed of a skeletal zombie. I moved down the stairs to stand with him hoping that our training would be enough to protect us. Would the witches scattered over town hear us if we tried to yell or would we just get the unwanted attention of the townspeople who would soon become casualties? We stood back-to-back, pressed against each other tightly so as not to let the monsters have the opportunity to separate us.

One of the abominations crawled over to me on nothing more than two feet, a pair of hands, and a head. I had no clue how its body was able to operate but then magic didn't have rules to follow, or at least none I was familiar with, and it didn't need to make sense. With one sneakered foot, I was able to kick it away from myself with a shriek that I hadn't intended on letting out. They had to make contact with the skin to get the soul and I was glad I had left the sandals at home. I could hear Damien behind me breathing heavily as he blasted a group of mini-monsters apart with his dark coin. A short distance away, I could see the creatures regroup using pieces and parts from their fallen comrades. They were a savage species and relentless.

"Any ideas on how to put them down and keep them there?" Damien asked short winded, and I thought back at what Gram had said, but I couldn't recall any information on how to destroy them. I would imagine if she had known, the Cretans wouldn't have killed so many of her friends. Some of the smaller skeletons were reassembling themselves into bigger monstrosities. So, they were resourceful too! Greeaaattt! I just hope they aren't too intelligent to strategize their attack.

"Just follow my lead and let's make a path!" I yelled over my shoulder as I kicked another walking rib cage with hands that had reached for my ankle and almost succeeded. Unfortunately, my skills only involved talking to deceased spirits, so I had to rely on my newfound defense moves, which weren't the best with such short attackers. I proceeded onward with my true love at my back continuing to blast away and helping me whenever I yelled back to him that I was bogged down. I didn't know how far we could make it, but I thought if we could just clear a path leading away from the front of the building, we might be able to make it to the store where we would have backup.

"Ha ha ha...!" laughed the cruel girl as she looked on at us desperately trying to get away from the army she had created. "You *are* weak. I should just finish you off here so that you can no longer bother my husband and muck-up his plans. I can't believe he ever saw you as a threat!" I knew she was trying to discourage me since I was the only one that could hear her but I tried to just block her out instead of giving her the pleasure of hearing me scream, 'shut up' in her general direction. Her voice sounded different, deeper, and with the deep rumble of someone much older than her.

Damien felt me tense up. "What's going on up there?" he asked, assuming that I had seen something he had not.

"She's just trying to shake me. I think she's with the Trickster. I don't know how they found us, but I hope the coven gets here soon!" The coven was more of an afterthought but I felt we had been gone for quite some time and they would be missing us by now. I just prayed they wouldn't be too late.

I crossed another crater in the sidewalk as we made our way to the road in hopes that we would be more visible to those down at the bait shop. More of the creatures had morphed together to form new, larger creatures that towered over even Damien's six-foot one frame. Their weakness was in the quick and incomplete stacking of bones that they were made up of, which I found could come crumbling down with just one kick to where the knee used to be.

"Oh, man, I don't think we're going to make it to the shop!" Damien yelled over his shoulder at me. I turned to see what new horror he was talking about, and I was mortified at the scene. More creatures were emerging from the gaps that had formed in the now demolished pavement. These monsters were different in that they had the peace of mind to bring weapons. Some just carried sharp sticks while others had long spears and bows (Hell must have been in short supply of innovations from this century). An arrow buzzed by my head as my fiancé shot another bolt of dark power at the oncoming attackers. The hairs on my arm began to stand up as a great amount of energy formed around us just as a spear was tossed at my chest. A war cry was let out that would have made any man proud as a plaid blur ran past us into the mist of our enemies. I knew it was Lillie right away and I was never as glad to see her as I was right then. Bertie and Crystal were right behind her and for the first time, I was able to see why Crystal was an asset to our quartet. She zipped by me with a sword that she had made forming energy around her into a sharp point, which was not an easy task, since she was also keeping us protected behind an invisible energy field. Damien and I stood back and just watched the experienced witches chop their way through the hoard in their various fashions. Multiple creatures were now retreating to their crevices; scurrying away on what few limbs they may have been able to retain. The ghost, knowing that her plans were now on hold, pouted at me in a way that finally showed her age before she raised her arms and disappeared on the breeze.

"She's gone, and I don't think she's too happy with us," I said to my Hero behind me. We both looked at one another and embraced. It was our first battle together and even though we wouldn't have been victorious without the help of the witches, we now had a taste of what we were up against, and we survived. We needed to report back and hopefully learn from our ordeal. There had to be a way we could put these creatures down for good!

"Leave 'em! They're running back to their hole in the ground," Bertie reported to the other members of the coven as she approached us. "You all okay?" she asked.

"We're glad you showed up when you did. We were about to have our butts handed to us," Damien tastefully said.

"What he said," I replied as I made my way quickly to the road, away from the devastated pavement, afraid that one lone hand might reach out of the crack and grab me like at the end of a horror movie. Once at a safe distance, I bent down with my hands on my knees trying to catch my breath. My heart was pounding; what a rush!

"Well, I'll say you all handled yourselves pretty well," Lillie snickered.

"I'm sure it had something to do with all the training this week." Damien smiled at her, and they shared a moment before Crystal interrupted.

"We better head back to the coven and report. These guys are notorious for sneaking up on you after they've regrouped." Crystal was thinking with a clear head, and she was absolutely right. We had to get back before Loki showed up so we could warn the others he was on his way. I remembered the ladies with us didn't have my gift for seeing the dead, so I relayed to them the dialogue between the pale girl and me. By the time I had finished my spiel, we had arrived back at the Bass Pole Bait and Tackle Shop. This time there was not a large group of men out front, and I mindlessly wondered who had won the chess game they had been so intently watching. I guess chess is more of a sport out in the country when there wasn't a hunting season in session. The female owner met us at the door.

"Off already? I was hoping to do some more swapping." She looked disappointed with her hands on her round hips. It must have been a slow day.

"Sorry, ran into something unexpected. How about we get a rain check on those crates we talked about?" Bertie explained while taking great giant strides towards the van. Crystal had gotten in already and Lillie was behind the wheel before Damien and I could get to the sliding door on the side. The other members whose names I had yet to retain were watching our backs as they quickly got in after us. The shopkeeper seemed to understand as she stood back and waved as we peeled out, a hard feat to accomplish in an old microbus.

We headed back to the abandoned restaurant that we had been calling home. Silence engulfed the interior of the vehicle as we left the small town and headed to the outskirts. I was sure we all were thinking the same thing; how had they found us? There was no way this Loki guy (or is it God, based on my research?) could have followed us, not in the unbelievably hard to hide semi-truck. The ghost girl could have hidden under our radar this whole time since no one had mentioned her before, but how did she get control of Loki's known minions? I only wished she could have dropped her name before she tried to kill us, but I knew that was asking for too much with our luck.

The familiar dirt road came up before I could put more thought into it, and we unbuckled ourselves in preparation to get out. Right away, I knew something was wrong.

No one came out of the restaurant to meet us and similar craters from in front of the library were now on the grounds of the old parking lot. The older witches defied all logic by jumping out of the van with the speed and grace of teenagers, leaving us behind to slide out of the back of the vehicle last. Damien and I didn't want to be so hasty after just being involved in a fight ourselves, so we were cautious as we exited and slowly moved around the van to face the big double doors of the building. The coven members that had been with us had already made their way inside where I assumed everyone must have been hiding, and we stood looking over the battlefield that was littered with the belongings of the followers. The tents that had been set up all over the front yard were now scattered to the four winds in different stages of destruction. The fire that normally burned tall all throughout the day and night had burned down to smoldering embers. Blood and corpses were the only things not scattered on the ground and I found restored hope. Damien nudged me in the direction of the door, and I knew he was anxious to see if everyone was okay.

The restaurant no longer looked like a meeting place for a large family to come together and enjoy a meal. Now it had the air of a field hospital set-up erratically and without the proper supplies for the injuries of those inside. For a camp full of women, I was surprised not to hear screams and sobs that should have met me at the door. Instead, I only heard orders being barked out by a familiar voice. I smiled at my Gram even though I was quickly scanning the room for all my friends and family. I made a mental note that Dawn was serving as a nurse to one of the Buck sisters as she wrapped one of her hands in a bandage. A crowd of women were standing in a corner with their faces turned upward, mumbling a chant or maybe a prayer to the ceiling. I didn't think the Tile God cared about what was going on under his roof. The followers had left their 'pale gray deity' in ill repair and had paid little or no attention to it, but isn't that the truth in all religions?

I continued to make a path to the back where another smaller crowd of women surrounded a single person that appeared to be humped over in the middle. My breath caught in my throat and what I had feared seemed to be true. Sarah's beautiful blonde hair was all I could see from where I was standing, frozen with fear to approach her and find that someone was dead. She held her hands over her face while multiple coven members caressed her shivering shoulders. I immediately realized who was missing from our courageous group. Damien was one step ahead of me and noticed the trouble almost as soon as I had entered the chaos. I could see he was currently questioning my Gram in quick hushed tones. I went to Sarah; I knew her well enough to know that she would need me more. She removed her hands from her eyes only long enough to recognize me before she plunged her face into my shoulder and her weeping intensified. I sat there in silence, stunned about the turn of events and trying like hell to hold it together for her.

It felt like we sat on the floor for hours, holding my best friend whose tears soaked through to my very soul. I hoped only to comfort her by being there in her most vulnerable moment. The ladies around us had dispersed to help the wounded, and Damien had gone outside to have a minute to collect himself. No one would have guessed this was going to happen. Even the Twins with their ears and eyes tuned into Hell had no clue about the surprise attack. I hadn't felt a ghost or a presence on the battlefield or in the building and neither did the other witches, so we knew the worst hadn't happened yet. It didn't change the fact that Steve was gone, taken by Loki's minions.

Chapter Twenty-One

THIRD STAGE OF GRIEF-BARGAINING

WHEN I could leave Sarah to go to Damien, I did. I discovered he was no longer out in front of the building. I heard a noise to my left, and I followed it to the back side of the abandoned restaurant where my fiancé was having a heated discussion with one of the twins. Tempers were still high, and everyone remained skittish, so I kept my distance back to avoid any miscommunication of my intent to listen in but not disturb their conversation.

"What have you heard? any news of my brother?" Damien asked visibly shaking back his anger.

"A little, but you're not going to like it," she replied. I could tell from Damien's shoulders that he had to restrain himself from reaching out and choking the witch. If she was smart, she would hurry and spill the beans before he lost control of himself.

"Regardless if I'll like it or not, you need to tell me what you know! NOW!" A lot of built-up rage came out in that last word, and I could see she noticed for the first time that they were alone. She looked around quickly to see if anyone else around could save her if he didn't like what she had to say, but I hid behind the wall, unsure if this was the appropriate time to reveal myself. He must have seen the fear she displayed but right now, all he cared about was his missing brother. "Please," he added to soften the mood and maybe help the witch get it out before he *really* lost control.

"Okay, but what I'm about to tell you, I haven't even told the girls yet." She looked one final time for help but she appeared less frightened then before. "I just received a message about your brother only moments ago and I haven't had time to process it just yet. I think Loki wants to set up a meeting to discuss his terms for the prisoner."

"Who?" Damien shook his head. Right, I hadn't had a chance to tell him that yet.

"The evil that's been after you, the one that caused all this," she motioned to the destruction around them. Damien shook his head again like it was full of bees.

"Okay, whatever. He's calling my brother a prisoner. That monster! No harm better come to him or I swear to God, it will be the last thing he ever does!" Damien's tone had risen again, and I half expected to see some of the coven come to her rescue, but they were still busy inside. "When does he want to meet? Where?"

"Now, I think." Her voice sounded little and unsure. "We replaced the protective barrier so he can't just waltz in here. He would have to be in the woods to avoid the circle." She snorted in a nervous way and then I could see her eyes grow big. "But Damien, I think he plans on trading Steve for Jo." I covered my mouth quickly to catch the shriek of surprise and watched as Damien leaned hard onto the cement wall. He ran his hand through his beautiful thick, dark hair and seemed to concentrate on the ground in silence.

"Don't tell them just yet, okay. I want Jo to hear it from me." She nodded in agreement, glad to finally be dismissed from his presence. She ran to the opposite side of the building from where I was hiding. Everything I had feared was coming true. I sighed; too loudly.

"You heard that, huh?" Damien responded. He didn't bother to turn around as I approached and stood in front of him. I had never seen him so distressed before. I felt solely responsible for what had happened to his brother, and I knew I could make everything alright if only I could find Loki before everyone else went looking. "No!" Damien said glancing at my face. "I know that look. You're thinking of sacrificing yourself for my brother, aren't you? There's always an alternative, Jo! Just let me think for a minute."

"Sweetie, you know I would do anything for you or Steve. Sarah and the two of you were the only family I had until a week ago and you all treated me like I belonged. I never felt such love and acceptance. I can't just sit idly by and do nothing. I have to protect that. The coven spent their lives trying to protect me and it was due to my Gram that they died in the line of duty. I can't live with that! I can't be like her!" I felt a tightness in my chest as I tried to hold back my tears. "I can make this end...I just have to give up." I choked up and could feel the burning emotions stinging the back of my thought as I held in a sob. This would be the end. Loki would never let me live once I told him I would never serve him. I needed to make my peace with God, there was no other way around this.

"Jo, I can't lose you too! I'm not giving up! You know this guy is never going to let *any* of us go after this. He probably knows that Sarah and I have powers now and what would stop him from trying to add us to his army? You go and we don't have a chance against him. You're our greatest weapon!" I would have said bargaining chip since that sounded more accurate, but I knew he would never see me that way, not even if it meant saving his brother.

"What else do you have in mind?" I asked gently stroking his hair as he wiped my tears away with his thumb.

"I don't know yet, but I think the sooner I meet with this 'Loki' and have this meeting, the better. I can't wait to give this SOB a piece of my mind!" I hugged him, hoping this wouldn't be the last time I could. I already had the knowledge that if things went sideways, I would offer myself anyway if it would spare Steve. I knew Damien wouldn't let me go alone or without a fight. I had to find a way to talk to Loki but without an enraged fiancé beside me to make things more difficult. This was one of those situations where I could use the help of my newfound family.

"Let's get back inside before we're missed, okay? I'm sure Sarah could use us right now." I took his hand and led him around to the front of the building. I glanced towards the woods, wondering if Loki was watching us and if he had Steve with him. We walked back into the once renowned Dairy Queen to find that everyone was in the same shape they had been in when we had snuck out. They had moved Sarah to one of the booths where she was in deep conversation with her mentor Sam. I assumed the twins had yet to tell anyone about the meeting that was about to go down between me and the Big Bad and I was thankful. It would give me a chance to talk privately with my Gram without a lot of stares from the other coven members.

I let go of my lover's hand and slowly walked over to where my Gram was stationed, barking orders as usual. I stared back at Damien for a long moment but he understood, I needed a second opinion, and he let me go as he continued to walk over to Sarah. As I approached my grandmother, I noticed the looks from the other witches but I wouldn't let it deter me. I patted her shoulder to get her attention and she turned quickly to meet me with a harsh look on her face that softened once she realized it was me. A thought came to me; this was a woman I never wanted to cross. I knew deep down that she would never hurt me, but I would never push that line.

"Yes, Josephine?" She inclined her head to the side and waited for my response.

"Ah, Gram, I need to speak to you outside, please."

"Can it wait, dear?" She was making sure that I knew she was in the middle of something, but I couldn't wait. I wanted Steve home ASAP.

"Not really, I'll wait for you out there." I left her standing there, unsure if she would blow me off or take me seriously. The dramatic walk away helped strengthen my statement and I didn't wait outside long. I only had a few precious seconds to be alone with my thoughts.

"Jo, you sounded serious, what is it?" She was taking a motherly tone with me this time but I knew she would be angry again soon enough.

"Loki wants to have a meeting. I think he's willing to make a trade for Steve's life." I could tell she was about to protest so I had to stop her quickly. "I'm not asking for your permission here, I'm prepared to do what's necessary if needed but I thought you might help me with insuring he won't double-cross us. I can't leave Damien with both a lost fiancé and a dead brother. He would never recover." I looked at her dead-on, afraid that breaking my eye contact would be a sign of weakness and at this moment, I couldn't afford to look meek. I wanted her to trust that I could do this without harm coming to the rest of the coven and my friends.

"You seem certain. I suppose I wouldn't be able to change your mind. I should at least accompany you on this suicide mission." I knew I would have no choice in the matter, but it was nice that she would let me think so.

"I don't know what to tell Damien. He thinks that we're coming up with a plan." I sighed and stared down at the ground beneath my feet.

"Well, it seems that you have a plan, dear, even if I don't agree with it." She placed a comforting hand on my shoulder and gave it a slight squeeze.

"My plan is simply giving up. It doesn't seem as much like a plan as it does an act of despair. I was kind of hoping you would talk to him while I sneak out the back to go meet Loki." I smiled at her with a half-cocked grin. I knew she wouldn't, but I just wanted a way to slip away with no muss, no fuss.

"Seems like the desperate act of someone who knows they're wrong." She did have a point there.

"I just don't think I can face him and be brave about it. I would rather he remember me as a self-sacrificing woman than the scared little girl that I'm trying to hide from you right now." That and I knew he wouldn't let me go and we were losing precious time. Gram's eyes shifted to something behind me and then back to mine.

"I'm sure *he* would love to hear this plan but I fear he might already be on a crash course to doing something stupid as we speak." Even as she said it, I realized there was a commotion going on in the woods behind the building that I hadn't noticed before. It sounded like trees cracking or bending more than they should. I had to move fast before he ruined everything.

I ran towards the noise, blind to everything else around me, stumbling over debris from the prior battle. If he got to Loki first, all would be lost and Steve might never come back to us alive. I leaped over a fallen log as I made my mad dash into the woods after the noise. It was like a giant had been released in the forest and it was making quick work of the trees. This particular monster would have made Paul Bunyan jealous as he had already cleared a path of at least two dozen spruces. I glanced downward at one of the fallen while still trudging forward, and I noticed that the trees were not cut by any blade but instead, each tree had scorch marks near the base where they had been blasted with enough force to push the pines over. Damien had really come into his own power since our arrival at the camp; and to think, just a month ago, he had been just plain old Damien to me.

I had to admit that I liked not being the only 'unusual' one in the relationship. I had distanced myself from the opposite sex from an early age. The dead didn't make appointments and guys could tell there was something off about me. The dead popped up at playgrounds or in classrooms and the kids started calling me 'the whispering girl'. Obviously it was due to the fact that they couldn't see me talking to anyone so it must have appeared as if I was talking to myself. It was one of the reasons I stopped talking to the dead and just ignored them, losing my gift in the process.

Damien was the second person I had told about my gift, Sarah being the first, and it had not been easy. I waited till after he told me he loved me for the first time. I never have good timing. I felt he needed to really know the person he proclaimed his love to before it was too late. We know how that turned out. I had made it to what appeared to be a sort of clearing and saw the man that I wanted to share my life with, that didn't resemble the man that proposed to me only months before. His face was red with anger and exhaustion. I could see faint lines across his beautiful cheek where branches must have grazed him. I wanted to go and hold him, but I was afraid I wouldn't be able to stop him. He would only push me out of the way like I wasn't standing there, not because of anything I had done, but for the things he couldn't help or change. I had only seen him this angry once before and when he got that way, there was no talking him down. I would just have to hope that the forest would be able to contain or withstand his anger and that he wouldn't destroy our chances with Loki.

I doubted this little display of power would surprise the once great God of the Norse. If anything, he was laughing at us right now from his hiding place. I watched as Damien blasted another tree to the ground and I could see the strain in his face, it was taking its toll. He staggered like a man on a bender and leaned on a nearby cedar for support. Seeing him in this weakened state made my heart ache and I knew this would be my opportunity to go to him. He would have to be more opt to listen to me now.

I approached him slowly, like he was a timid creature that might turn tail and run at the sound of a stranger coming. He was more like an injured mountain lion I was afraid may see me as a threat. I made it around to the front of him and saw his face was wet with tears. My arms ached to hold and comfort my true love, but he turned away from me before I could. It wasn't meant to be offensive, he lived in a world where men weren't supposed to cry, at least not in the presence of a woman that respected him. I didn't share in his belief and his heartfelt display of emotion only made me love him more.

"You should have waited for me. We could have destroyed the woods together." I smiled up at him, hoping my small joke would help stop the tears from coming.

"I've never felt so lost," he said distantly.

"Well, camp is just back that way," I motioned towards the direction of the coven. I knew that wasn't what he meant, but I was desperately trying to ease the tension.

"You're kidding, right?" he asked sarcastically. I silently prayed that he wasn't planning on taking out his despair on me as I dropped my arms to my sides, knowing no embrace was coming. We didn't have time for this show of lumberjack rage. There were more pressing matters ahead. Loki wouldn't wait forever and Steve was still out there waiting to be saved. I was frustrated with Damien now and this wasn't going to end well.

"Damien, what do you want me to say? We've lost!"

"I'm not letting him win, not without putting up one hell of a fight!" he yelled.

"I won't let you, or Sarah, or even Steve fight my battles for me. He wants me and he can have me if that means that all this nonsense will FINALLY be over!" I was seriously pissed and I placed my hands on my hips for emphasis. He would have to do nothing short of knocking me out to change my mind on this one. He wouldn't dare of course.

"This sounds more like an ultimatum than a discussion. Shouldn't I get a say in who my future wife gives her soul to? Call me old fashioned, but I do remember you promising to be with *me* forever and now you want to go back on your promise." I tried closing my eyes tight to picture that day I said yes over a picnic lunch. It seemed so long ago but it stifled my anger.

"I will love you forever and nothing will change how I feel." I touched his face tenderly. "But you already knew that, didn't you?" I smiled and I could see my reflection shining back at me through his beautiful blue eyes, glistening with unshed tears. I wiped away the one tear that escaped his long, dark lashes.

"I know I can't stop you, but I can't let you go alone. You know this guy won't be alone either." He reached out and held my hand, enclosing it in his rougher, warm palm.

"As long as you behave, you can come along." I booped his nose with one finger and helped him off the tree to a standing position. That seemed to satisfy him, but I knew he would still be unpredictable once Loki was near. Especially since I was who he really wanted. I was scared, admittedly, but Damien's hand in mine was a comfort I needed.

There was a rustle behind us as hushed voices rose over the fallen logs. Just as I feared, Loki was planning on double-crossing us! I braced against Damien, prepared to fight, when a familiar voice arose above the others.

"Get the lead out, ladies!" Lillie yelled over her shoulder at the entourage she had brought with her. Suddenly the woods were full with the sounds of the coven coming to our aide. I should have known the Buck sisters wouldn't be able to zip their lips forever. The group encircled us with Dawn leading the pack that was now blocking our path forward. She smiled at us as she came into view.

"You didn't think I would let you make this mistake without me, did you? You haven't even begun your training, so naturally you would be useless without *my* help," she said matter-of-factly. Despite the arrogance, I had never been so happy to see her. I had been so busy bonding with these lovely ladies, I had forgotten that they were also my protectors. My family.

"I'm sorry dear, but I had to tell the others. Don't be cross with them." Gram stood at the back of the group, her gray head barely noticeable over all the others.

"No, Gram, you did what you had to do. I'm happy you have all come, but I don't think Loki will be."

"Who cares what that old buzzard wants? He won't be getting you, girl, I can promise you that!" Marty proclaimed. I beamed at all of them, especially Sarah who I could see was making her way to the front of the group behind us. She walked over to me slowly with her head down and I met her halfway and threw an arm around her shoulders. My thoughts were brought back to Steve and where he could be. If Loki really did intend to make a trade for me, then Steve would be with him. There had to be a way to ensure that he wouldn't try to double-cross us. I didn't want to let my friends down by losing Steve for good and possibly my life. I needed to think of something fast, before Loki caught wind of all of us in the woods waiting for him.

"Sarah, I hate to ask, but is it possible for you to do me a favor?" Sarah looked up to me with tear filled eyes. She nodded her head a little too quickly and the crystalline drops spilled on to her pale cheeks. I wish I could have done it without her, but she was familiar with Steve's energy pattern. He would be seen as a low rating compared to Loki and I knew that it would be a safe thing she could do to help while keeping her at a distance from the action. I replayed my thoughts to her and she nodded her head. I didn't think she had yet found her voice to speak and her trembling body confirmed it, but she walked away from the group and deeper into the woods.

"Let's take a moment here and really think this through, Jo. You know Loki isn't just going to give Steve over to us. We like him too, but we can't win this war without you. There is no reason to even consider his offer. It is nothing but lies dreamt up by the devil himself!" Dawn was really adamant about her feeling towards our common enemy and I hadn't expected anything less from her. I had feared they had come to the woods to find and stop me and I knew that was still their hope. In just the week I have been here, they had come to know that I would never leave a friend behind, much less a family member. Steve was family too and I would never forgive myself for standing idly by and allowing someone to take his life for mine.

"You guys have been so accepting, so amazing, and I know you have this belief that I am this big savior, but I am not. I am just a girl going through the motions until I graduate. I am a kid for, Christ's sake! I miss the days when my only problems consisted of the dead hounding me. Now I have the task that my dead mother has left to me. I will never be strong enough or powerful enough for him. This could all be over for all of you if I just went with him. No more coven threats or lives lost in risk of protecting me."

"What are you saying, Jo?" Dawn asked.

"I'm just saying that you are all very brave for coming here to help after what you have already been through. There is no need for more bloodshed. Don't you see? You can all go back to your normal lives and just forget this." I wanted nothing more for them than to live long and productive lives. I was expecting this little speech to go better, but it didn't seem as though any of the coven were going to budge.

"Come on, deary. You didn't really think we were going to let you do this alone, did you? We have devoted our lives to protecting this family line from the likes of evil. These women have left their families in order to be here." Gram's words were met with howls and hollers from the others who were all in agreement.   Surely   now   our   cover was blown. Still, the sound was comforting and some of the guilt I had been carrying around lifted, much like their voices on the evening breeze. These grown women had come into this with the knowledge that their lives were at stake and still they met me on the hillside, ready for battle. I no longer saw them as weak or old, but warriors of a different breed. They had done all of this with courage and I needed that lesson now more than ever.

"Well, you all seem very confident in how this will turn out, but a meeting is all Loki is looking for now. A meeting with him could mean this all will end. A friend would be returned, and a prisoner would be replaced with another. It is time for me to sacrifice as you all have already. It may not even come down to that, who knows?"

"Jo, you don't know what lies ahead. You are not ready for him yet!" Lillie looked at me with eyes filled with worry and I knew she was right. What little I had learned about Loki at the library wouldn't help me if it came down to a fight against him.

"Margie is the only one that has gone up against him and lived. They fought one-on-one while she was on her way to get you." Sam's statement was met with agreement from the others and a path formed as Gram made her way closer to me.

"He's very strong, but he hides behind the facade of a normal man with the strength of something powerful. During our engagement, I noticed that he fought with hesitation, and he spoke with the sound of two different voices. Being a woman who is around the spirits all the time, I know the sound of a possessed man when I hear one. Loki must have crawled out of hell with nothing more than his spirit intact and he has embodied this poor man. He won't be as strong as he once was, which would explain his need for an army to carry out his evil business. We need more time so I can get an exorcism kit together. At his weakened state, we may be able to banish him back to hell!" My grandmother is a tough cookie, I cannot imagine anyone else surviving what she went through. It took a moment to consider her advice, but I knew that time wasn't a luxury we had. Any more of it wasted would be a red flag to Loki, and he might kill poor Steve.

"Loki is expecting a trade. How do you suppose we trick him into doing an exorcism instead? I need to go up there, or he is going to get suspicious. I will think of something to give us more time."

"We need to check on Sarah. Come on gals; get your rears in gear!" Sam exclaimed over her shoulder as she proceeded to go towards the hill that Sarah had disappeared behind. I followed hoping that Sarah had received intel that could help us. We rounded the top and saw Sarah talking to Sam who had been training her these last few days. Their heads were together in a way that reminded me of fellow teammates in a huddle, discussing their next move to play. Sarah raised her head and looked at me over the other woman's shoulder. The look in her eyes confirmed what I already feared. Still, I needed no assumptions holding me back, I had come for straight answers.

"Did you find out what we needed?" I asked, preparing myself for the bad news.

"I don't feel Steve anywhere; neither does Sam. With our combined ability, we have been able to reach the town. A circle that big should have touched Steve wherever he has been hidden. What if they have killed him and that's why I can't feel him? Jo, what will I do without him?" Her eyes welled up again and Sam placed a comforting hand on her shoulder. I went to my friend and hugged her tightly. Damien joined in by reaching around me and holding the both of us. I longed to stay in-between the warmth of the both of them, but I was on a mission and the anger I had rising up in me helped to release my hold. I wiped the tears from my cheeks with the back of my hand. I squared my shoulders and put on a brave face.

"It's settled then. He never planned to come here for a trade and I won't leave with him without Steve."

"What do you have in mind, dear?" Gram asked having just joined our party. It was nice, her letting me take the reins for once.

"It will be hard to surprise him since he is the one that set the meeting up, but I bet he doesn't know that we know about Steve. We will have to use that to our advantage." Come to think of it, that was the only advantage we had over a million-year-old deity. "I go alone, but with you all watching from a distance." I knew they wouldn't allow me to go solo, but at a safe distance, I wouldn't have to worry so much about them. I noticed some were nodding their heads yes so I proceeded.

"At the library, I learned a few things about our enemy that I think will help negotiations. If I think that the conversation is going poorly, I will signal for you and you can charge in, guns blazing. I just want to try talking to him first." That statement was partially true and I hoped it was believable. No one, not even Damien, knew what new information I had scouted out on the internet mostly because we hadn't had time to discuss those findings. I was thankful I hadn't spilled the beans yet since basically my search had been useless.

After a long pause in which I held my breath waiting for an argument, I heard, "she is so stubborn, are ya sure she's related to you?" Marty cocked her head in Gram's direction and I saw the old lady finally give me a smile that went all the way up to her eyes. I hope the reaction was from pride and not her way of saying, "no way in hell am I going to let you do this alone, but I'll humor you." The joke did help the rest of the crowd who were looking so serious at this point. I knew Gram was the lady running the show but for a brief moment, I felt the most grown-up that I had ever felt. Never before had anyone allowed me to take over and make the decisions. In a foster home, you hear a lot of nos. If no had been a commodity, we would have been rolling in dough. Still, I learned that everyone else knew what was best for me and I should just go with it without making much of a fuss. I was actually missing that. I wasn't getting much of a fight here, but in a small way that was still a victory in my favor.

Chapter Twenty-Two
NOT YOU, AGAIN!
Frank

THE trucker hated waiting out in the woods. His body was still throbbing from the last encounter he had and not with adrenaline, but with aches he didn't even want to think about. He could sense the dog's great mass hiding behind a boulder as instructed by the voice. They didn't want to take the chance of the beast killing someone before it was time. Frank had seen for himself what the dog could do to a person just because that someone had taken a look at it. Most didn't seem to even notice the giant dog, and would make a wide berth for him whenever they walked by. It was almost as though they could feel the evil that surrounded the hell hound, and they didn't want to touch it.

Most didn't even look in their direction at all but one poor, sorry sap, had gotten himself a looky-loo. You could tell that the dog was visible to him by the almost funny look on his face. His eyes got cartoon-sized and seemed to bulge out of his head. Mr. Holtz knew whatever the voice knew when it came to the dog and other things unknown, if the voice allowed it. The trucker and the voice shared thoughts as well as a body. It seemed to him, the brain intruder had not expected what came next as the businessman of sorts started to scream this high pitched yelp, and fell to the ground, dead. His arms, which only held one briefcase, reached up towards his face as his mouth made an "O" look. He reminded Frank of that famous painting that guy with one ear made of the night sky. Lucky for them, the town had been unusually quiet since they had arrived to look for some girl, and not too many people noticed the man crumbling to the ground clutching his chest. Apparently, according to the voice's memories, this was a rare occurrence to witness.

He also knew that Loki had a soft spot for the wolf, almost as though he were kin to it. It was an odd feeling to have towards a pet but he knew the difference. He himself had experienced love for another person at one time or another. All that was before the voice, and it seemed like a distant memory now. Loki had shown no pity for the man, even as he lay dead. So many people had forgotten about Hell and the creatures it contained, so few could see the unknown. Many just didn't want to know about the things Frank had seen, things that whisper in the night and can suck your soul right out.

The voice hushed him, it was deep in thought, and the trucker couldn't see what it was up to. Sometimes the voice could block him out of his own head, making it hard for Frank to stop the visitor in any way. It would take over his body easily without hesitation if Frank tried to resist him. Mr. Holtz liked his body, and enjoyed the use of it. To have someone else pulling the strings made him feel like a puppet. He was tired of the voice, in body and in spirit.

It had left him alone for a while after the accident 20 some odd years ago, and he thought he was finally rid of it. He discovered that it was only lying dormant, waiting for its time again to take over. He couldn't think of when that had been. When the voice took over, he lost all track of time. The voice felt that time was irrelevant but Frank kept trying to appeal to it. He had deliveries to make. Companies wouldn't just pay for his gas to go on this killer adventure without a delivery in mind. The visitor had no concept of money, its thoughts were always on bad things. Even now, the master, Frank hated calling it that, was deep in thought over battle strategies. It thought in images of a chess board and pieces made of people. Frank wondered which one of the pawns was him. He fancied himself as a castle, free to move back and forth unseen. He liked being off to the side.

He hated the things that he had to do for the nuisance in his head, but he was thankful he hadn't been caught yet. He didn't see himself doing well in prison and to be convicted of a murder he didn't remember doing was just insane. Maybe prison wouldn't be so bad, it would restrain him from committing any more crimes unknowingly. The voice may even finally leave him if it had no way to get to the things it desired.

If only he could get more time alone to think about how to make the body thief go away. Only when the intruder was in thought, did Holtz have free reign over his body, but most of that time was brief. He was afraid that his mind wouldn't hold out much longer if he didn't get away. 'What if I get rid of it and it just finds someone else to inhabit?' he thought. The trucker didn't wish his curse on his worst enemy, but he had to take care of himself and worry about the rest later.

A shudder went through the driver as he spread his arms wide to stretch his aching muscles. He had grazed the protective boundary earlier with one hand that now hurt, and Frank stuck it in his mouth like a small child would after a cut finger. He hated this stupid insane stuff. How can something you can't see hurt you? Of course, he knew the answer from the inhabitant in his brain, but he wished he could be ignorant again.

The soul suckers from under the ground had been new to him. He couldn't have imagined in his wildest nightmares that he would be manning an army of creatures that have the ability to suck your soul clean out just by touching your skin! He didn't know about a soul stealing dog from Hell, either. He remained surprised every time Loki called on some new minion to do the work Frank was incapable of doing.

The voice in his head gave a little surge at the mention of 'its' name, even though Frank had only thought it. Maybe the voice could be removed like a Bloody Mary thing. He would just have to say its name out loud three times into a mirror and maybe it would vanish. The mental visitor checked Frank's memory to find out what the Bloody Mary reference was only to find that it was only what they called an "urban legend". Frank thought about Beetle Juice and that kept the visitor busy for another minute or two. Once the voice was satisfied that Frank didn't have any information that could get rid of him, it went back to thinking about his hostage in the wings. He had left strict instructions for the soul eaters not to harm the guy called Steve, but that didn't mean they would listen. Loki hated having to borrow monsters from the Devil but he often applauded Loki's work and was easily persuaded into helping him.

The Devil enjoyed watching him create chaos upon the Earth and anything Loki could do, would help Hell in the long run. Convincing the Traveler (whoever that guy was) to let them borrow the Dog had been harder. The Traveler traditionally stayed out of the affairs of both humans and gods, according to the memories Frank got from the voice. He preferred to wait by the sidelines to see who would come out victorious. Loki on the other hand, loved helping to tip the scales in the favor of evil. It was even more rewarding that he had conquered a once good man, and had turned him into a killer against his will. Frank could feel that he was Loki's favorite conquest since his return to the livings' plane. Holtz had been easy when he had expected more of a challenge, but the girl was his real challenge. She would be harder to convince to change sides, but he had his bargaining chip waiting to be rescued in the outer ring of Hell.

Loki knew Jo's weak spot was her friends. She especially seemed to like the dark haired male. The soul eaters had been told to capture the taller of the males but they couldn't find an opportunity to get him when he was alone. When she and the tall male left, leaving the others behind unguarded, it gave them the opportunity to strike. The creatures had no respect for Loki because the Devil was their true leader. He wasn't used to not being feared by his followers, but things had changed since he had been dead. The world had moved on without him, and had left him a shell of his former self. If Jo would only join him, he could get back some that he had lost! She would build him an army that would never tire and never hunger, an army whose only purpose would be to serve him. He would teach her how to put the spirits of the dead into walking bodies that would be better and stronger than anything he could borrow from Hell.

If Loki had had lips at that moment, they would have been dripping with saliva at the thought of ruling the world with a force made up of the dead. As if on cue, Frank wiped his mouth with the back of his hand. Frank hated how in sync he had become with the invader but it was like a roommate he couldn't get rid of. He could hear the dog switch positions as if it had been alerted to some unknown sound, and it put Frank and Loki on the alert as well.

The trucker prayed that the talks would be quick; he knew how Loki liked being dramatic and drawing things out.

They still had a delivery to drop off and time was a-wastin'. A twig snapped in the distance and Frank threw his arm out towards the Dog as a signal not to move. The dog, like the creatures, had a master that it took orders from and it didn't take too kindly to all the demands Loki had been making. They both hoped that this meeting with the girl wouldn't turn into a big waste of time if the animal ate those they needed.

The sun going down on the forest offered them the only light it had left as Frank moved into position to welcome the girl they had waited so long to meet in person. Frank wondered again what made this girl so special and how she was going to help them raise an army. The trucker wasn't too thrilled with the idea of commanding the undead, but he held onto the hope that the voice would let him go after this last job. Little did he know, the voice had been able to hide many of his plans from Frank's inferior mind, and it planned on keeping him until his body was no longer of use to him.

Frank could see the silhouette of someone approaching as he moved further away from the safety of the boulder, where the beast still hid. The sound was still within the protective border. Frank's skin felt like it was sizzling standing so close to the border, but the voice had taken control of him and there was nothing he could do but let go. He could see the top of the girl's head as she came up the hill and Frank's mouth opened to say, "Don't you move, unless I instruct you to, beast! We need this one to stay alive." Frank could have sworn he saw the animal smirk, if dogs could make such an expression, and turn its massive head away from the approaching female. She was now practically standing in front of them and Holtz glanced around to insure she had come alone.

"Don't worry, I'm alone, but I must warn you that if this doesn't go down just right, my friends aren't far behind me." The girl bravely stood before them, her bosom heaving from the hike up the hill. Frank tried not to stare.

"You try anything, and the boy will die a slow and painful death." Deep down the voice hoped the boy was still alive so he had something to trade at all.

"Yeah, about that; where is Steve? What have you done with him?" She looked very angry and the real Frank, deep down, admired her for it. Loki on the other hand was concerned that somehow she knew they didn't have the boy with them. He hoped that she would come just a bit closer so he could reach out and just take her. It would be so quick, no one would have a chance to raise the offense. Loki thought it clever to step back a pace as if her anger had moved him in hopes that she would come closer. She didn't move, instead, she crossed her arms over her breasts as if to shield them from Frank's stare. Loki jerked his head upwards. It was only her power he wanted.

"I will show you the boy in time, when I know you're ready to make the decision that will set him free. You do know what I want, don't you?" He smiled at her and the trucker's yellowed teeth made the gesture even more grimacing.

"Don't play games with me, L-o-k-i." She said his name slow, emphasizing every syllable and he shuddered. The trucker still silently hoped she would say it two more times quickly, and the intruder would be gone for good. "I know who you are, I've even met your wife. I will vanquish her if Steve comes to any harm. I have left instructions for her to be brought here if things go wrong and I promise you, the witches will not hesitate; kind of like how you didn't hesitate to kill my family!" The trucker swallowed loudly and he tried to think of who he had killed that this child could've belonged to.

She looked to be in her twenties so it would have had to have been around that time. A light bulb went off over Frank's head and he remembered a crash on a deserted stretch of road. He recalled a station wagon and the sound of a crying infant. Could this be that infant? Loki had control of the trucker's body so the thoughts going through his head didn't show on his face. Loki hushed the man, he didn't want to be interrupted while he was strategizing. What about this wife she mentioned?

Maybe Jo thought she might have the upper hand in this argument? She seemed to have caught Loki off guard and the loud gulp had misled her to believe so. This had to be rectified. Loki laughed long and loud and the sound of it caused the birds to fly off in a whisper of wings that stirred the growing darkness. Jo was taken aback but she tried not to look visibly shaken. Perhaps the laugh reminded her of a certain scarred faced man that had been appearing to her. Frank thought he saw a chill run through her body.

Loki interrupted her thoughts by saying, "You know nothing of the things I do. When you join us, you will learn many things about me. Know that I care not for the things that my wife does nor do I care about what happens to her in the lives that follow! Her story is her own and I don't plan on discussing it with you! You have only one thing I want and that I feel is a fair trade for your mortal. Now, what say you to that?" Frank almost laughed at that last line because he was reminded of an old Woody Allen movie he had watched as a younger man. Although Frank was finding humor in what was going on, Loki was not as happy. He hadn't liked the comments made about his wife and her encounter with the girl. He had no idea she was trying to help him and deep down he admired her strength. Last he saw of her, she had tried to escape with him from the grips of Death where only gods went when they died. She hadn't been as powerful as him and her hand had disappeared from his as he made the final gate into this world. He had been melancholy for many years after being separated from the only creature that had ever understood him for what he was. Then he found Frank Holtz and he knew what he had to do to get her back.

With his own army, he could storm in and take her by force. Now that he knew she was free, he wouldn't have to rush his plans and reveal himself too early to the other deities. He would have to find her, but for now, he would deal with this girl. He had been waiting for her response and it seemed she was still contemplating her answer. She switched her weight from one foot to another, chewing on her bottom lip, and then she looked up at him under dark long lashes that framed brown eyes.

"I do know many things about you, Loki, indeed. I know what you want me for and I'm going to tell you now, it's not possible. I've been training for a week and I have just learned how to listen to the dead again. I could never do what my mother did. What do I have to offer then, you ask? Well, I do have someone that can train me but she won't if I have already pledged my allegiance to your side. If only you would give me time to become what you want, I can be what you need. You would of course have to release Steve before I would agree with such a notion." Jo was flying by the seat of her pants on this one, Frank thought. Perhaps she had been thrown off by Loki's lack of interest in knowing that his wife had appeared or she was hoping she would get more of a rise from him. Either way, Frank couldn't believe that she was agreeing to work with Loki.

The voice thought long and hard about the girl's proposition. He had known she was weak, that was part of the appeal to come after her before she was too powerful. Should he allow her to be trained by some mortal and then he can come and pluck her from the vine a ripe grape, instead of a seedling? The idea sounded too good to be true but how did he know for sure she wouldn't run?

"I don't think it would be wise for me to give up my bargaining chip so soon. I think I will keep him around for a little longer; he seems sweet. Maybe we should just eat him up! You forget who I am, girl! I don't take demands lightly!" Loki didn't want his godlike pride to be broken by some common child of man. Still, he liked the idea of someone else spending time with the girl, training her for him. He only wanted her power, to work for him not against him. "But, your suggestion is appealing to me. How about I make a new deal with you, human? I keep your friend, safe, at home with me; and you come back to me in one month. I'll be watching all the while from the shadows, or in your dreams. If I see anything I don't like, I will bring him here and let you all watch me tear him limb from limb." He smiled his evil crooked grin again at her and she trembled slightly again.

The girl thought the idea over a moment longer then said, "You drive a hard bargain, Loki, but I see you have the upper hand. I'll expect Steve to be return in the same condition that you took him in if this deal will work."

"Of course, no harm will come to the boy, but I should think you would be more worried about yourself."

"See, now you don't know anything about me, do you? I will be back here in one month after the sun sets, and if I don't see Steve, the deals off." The girl took another step back as a precautionary measure to insure that Loki wouldn't just reach within the protective barrier and grab her right then and there. "You will hold your minions back until then as well?"

Loki liked that she was so suspicious of him, it showed great intelligence. This girl may prove to be invaluable to him after all, in more ways than one. "I would give you my word of honor, but somehow I know that will not be good enough. Know that I would not jeopardize my plans just for a little revenge on the witches. But if I am disappointed, I cannot insure you or your friends' safety."

"I understand, but I hope you know that I don't control what the coven does. I can only insure you that I plan on exploring my powers so that I may be able to do what you ask." Frank secretly admired her attitude.

"That should be good enough for now. I think this is the beginning of a grand relationship, don't you think?" Loki looked at her smugly through Frank's eyes and the trucker hoped that he wouldn't do anything foolish to botch things up.

"I think I don't have any say-so in this relationship, so no. I would not call that grand. A relationship should be open and not secretive but I feel you have a lot of secrets you haven't shared." Loki had to applaud her courage to speak to a god in such a way but she was right. He had many a secret, but now was not the time.

"Maybe under different circumstances we could be better confidantes, but for now we must trust one another to do what is best for your friend. I feel that you comprehend my advantage and that you will do the right thing. I must leave you now to your training and trust my minions will not dispose of your male." The trucker turned and began his hike back to his rig which he had left next to the road into town. He signaled to the beast which fell into step next to him.

Chapter Twenty-Three:
TRAINING ANYONE?
Jo

I stood speechless at the sight of the massive dog having not seen it hidden behind the boulder. I shivered with the knowledge that there may be other creatures waiting for me out in the dark if I hadn't agreed to Loki's deal. Maybe they were still waiting silently, hoping to disembowel me with just a signal from the trucker's hand.

I held my head high as I came down off the hill. I wanted to give them the appearance that I had fought gallantly for the life of our friend and that our negotiations had went well. Really, deep inside I was trembling. Seeing that massive creature, and fearing that there were more hidden all around us, had frightened me. I thought it was reasonable fear. Isn't that what monsters did? Their only purpose in life was to terrify us of the dark and feed off our fears. I knew the creatures in the shadows were getting a full belly from the fear I was projecting but I wanted to appear brave.

I had stood up to Loki the best I could because Steve and Sarah were counting on me. I planned on going up that hill and handing myself over to Loki. Thank God I was able to come up with a better plan on the spot. I saw Damien from the corner of my eye approaching me. To convince Loki that I had surrendered but play up the fact that I was unfit to carry out his task was plan B. Loki had fallen for it, giving us more time to come up with a better plan and to train so that I can fight back. Still, in the back of my mind, I knew I would do what I had to when the time came. If it meant sacrificing myself, so be it, otherwise, I planned on going down fighting. Time for thinking was over as Damien approached, waiting for me to tell him something.

"Still alive," I said smiling up at him.

"That I can see. What happened up there?" he asked quickly, grabbing me up in his arms in an embrace.

"He said he would give me a month to become what he wants. Then he will be willing to trade Steve for me." I was hoping that would be enough for now, for I was exhausted of looking brave for everyone else but I knew Damien's concerns would not end there.

"A month will give us enough time to launch an offensive strike on him. Did he mention where my brother was being kept?"

"He just said that his minions were keeping him alive. I don't know where yet. We'll get him back, Damien, I promise. Whatever it takes, I'm going to get him back." I stroked one of his massive arms to comfort him and he only continued to hold me. Our moment alone was brief, and then we were surrounded by a dozen worried faces. I saw Sarah emerge from the back of the mob to stand next to Damien who put a comforting arm around her. I released him and went to stand by Sarah's other side. The ladies were obviously waiting for me to say something and now would be as good a time as any to address them all.

"Don't look so worried, ladies! Steve will be released in one month so this is a win for us! Our enemy promises to stop any more attacks on our coven which will be a big improvement to our training time..." I could see many sceptical faces staring at me now and I wasn't surprised to see my Gram step out from among the crowd.

"So he went with plan B, huh?" Straight to the point as always, my Gram.

"He's giving us a month and his word that no harm will come to Steve," I replied shortly. "Now, let's all get back to the base before he changes his mind. We can talk more there if we must." I waved my arms as a signal that we should all be moving and I even made it a few steps towards the distant building before another voice emerged.

"Jo, wait up!" Dawn trotted up beside me slightly out of breath. "So he's going to leave us to train you? No strings attached?"

"I'm hurt that you feel my negotiation skills aren't up to snuff. The real question here is will a month be long enough? Do you think you can teach me what I need to know to beat him?" She stopped suddenly and for the first time, I saw a smile crack across her lips.

"I'm sure as hell going to try. You better get plenty of rest, girly. Come tomorrow, the real work starts." I knew I was up for the challenge.

LOOK FOR BOOK TWO OF THE COVEN OF SECRETS, LOVE AND POWER

Acknowledgements

To my mom that told me to stop being a little witch and put on my big girl pointy shoes and get this published, thanks for always pushing me to be the author of my own story.

Much appreciation to my little sis that never complained of proofreading every page no matter how many times I changed it.

To all my friends and loved ones that have listened to me pitch this book for years and never stopped asking me for the next, bless you. Without you all in my life, I would have never found my audience.

Special thanks to Amanda and her husband for their hard work and beautiful cover that made this book possible, and to their company, Pixels and Pens, that felt I was worthy of being published. You gave me a legacy I can leave for my little witches.

Lastly, thank you the readers for whom I hope to continue to make the impossible possible even if it's just fiction.

Printed in Great Britain
by Amazon